The Valentine Wager

The Valentine Wager

A Lange Brothers Romance

Nan Reinhardt

TULE
PUBLISHING

Dedication

For my dear friend and retired police officer, Larry J. Thanks for helping me keep it real with your invaluable advice and information, and thank you for your 37.5 years of service to the city of Indianapolis.

Chapter One

KITT BOYNTON SCOWLED as the driver heading right for her veered off to his own lane before laying on his horn and making a terribly rude gesture. The second time it had happened in as many kilometers...er, miles on the road down to the center of town. "*Eejit!*" she shouted and returned the gesture. Closed up in the car as she was, there was no way he heard it; nonetheless, it felt good to release her frustration. Were the people in this town dense or just truly poor drivers? She really wasn't fond of driving in Indiana.

Carefully, she maneuvered her cousin Bren's Jeep around a curve and the little town of River's Edge nestled on the banks of the Ohio River came into view. Thank the Lord, she was almost there. Who knew traveling the short distance from the Four Irish Brothers Winery on the ridge above town to their in-town tasting room would be so hazardous? Another mile and she'd turn on—she glanced at her phone propped up by the gearbox—Riverview Road. Then a few blocks to the tasting room. Dry frosty leaves blew across the road as she passed a rocky outcropping where a lovely little waterfall spilled into a shallow pool below. She wondered why it wasn't frozen as cold as it gotten since Christmas.

Southern Indiana reminded her a bit of Ireland, which in turn made her homesick for County Wexford and Ma and Da and her brothers and sisters—all seven of them—and the horses. The time difference was six hours, so it would be nearly six P.M. on the horse farm where Kitt had grown up. Da would be feeding the livery horses—pouring grain and dropping flakes of hay. Her heart ached at the thought of Dewey, her Irish hunter gelding, nestled in his stall, probably wondering why she wasn't there to ride him across the meadow and down to the sea. She hoped her little sister Nora was riding him as she'd promised.

A siren wailed briefly and when she glanced in the rear-view mirror, red and blue lights flashed behind her. A police car needed to get around. Why didn't he just swing into the opposite lane and go past? There was nothing coming. *Whaaaa-wha-wha.* The siren whooped again and now the guarda's car was right on her bumper. Was he pulling her over? She checked her mirror again. He was!

Frustrated, Kitt scouted for a safe place to stop, finally ending up pulling into an empty lot next to the post office. Her speed had been perfectly within the legal limit posted, Bren had checked that all the lights and signals on his Jeep were working fine, and the tires were brand new. What could this guy possibly want? The officer pulled in crossways behind her, blocking her in the parking space, but he didn't jump right out of his car. Instead, he sat there for a moment, staring at something in his lap.

Finally, he opened his door and got out. In her side-view

mirror, she watched him approach the Jeep. He was big. Intimidatingly tall, and under his winter jacket, the buttons on his navy-blue uniform shirt strained a bit across his brawny chest. He wasn't wearing a hat and his hair was all shades of blond and light brown with glints of gold, styled deliberately messy, more like an Aussie surfer dude than a small-town copper. The only thing missing was a pair of mirrored sunglasses, which she was certain were probably on the passenger seat of his police car. He looked like the type.

When he drew nearer, she could see he was what her sister Maeve would call *a fine thing*—clean-shaven and ruggedly handsome with full, sensual lips. He eyed her license plate as he tapped on an electronic device with a stylus. She took a deep breath and rolled down the window.

"License, registration, and proof of insurance, please." His voice was deep and oh, dear God, poured over her like warm melted butter with just those few impersonal words. His gray eyes reminded her of the Irish Sea right before a storm.

Whew. She must be lonelier than she thought. Those were *not* the kinds of comparisons she ought to be making at this moment.

Digging around in the glove box, she produced the black pouch Brendan had told her was there and found the registration and insurance certificate. Then she reached toward her capacious handbag on the floor in front of the passenger seat.

"Hands on the wheel, please." The officer's clipped words stopped her mid-reach.

"D'ye want to see my driving license?" She looked over her shoulder at him bent over and peering into the car. "It's in my bag"—she pointed—"down there."

He nodded brusquely. "Bring out your wallet, slowly."

She swallowed the chuckle that rose in her throat as she pulled her wallet out, opened it, and offered it to the policeman.

"Remove the license from your wallet, please," he ordered.

She did and handed it to him. "Officer, what's going on?"

He held up one finger as he examined it. "This is an Irish license."

Handsome, but a bit thick? "Perhaps because I'm just arrived from Ireland?"

He raised one blond brow. "Well, Miss Boynton, do you know why I stopped you?"

She had no idea why he'd stopped her. She shrugged. "Not a clue, I'm sure."

"Have you been drinking, ma'am?"

This time she laughed out loud. "Are ye quite mad, man? It's not even noon."

He eyed her, his gray eyes going from charcoal to silver in the late-morning light. "I ask because you were driving rather erratically and on the wrong side of the road."

Kitt scoffed. "*I* was driving erratically? You should be chasing down the two eejits back there." She pointed over her shoulder as she peered at his brass badge glinting in the noon sun. No name, just a badge number. "One of them nearly plowed me over."

He sighed and straightened. "Miss Boynton, please step out of your vehicle."

She tilted her head, trying to see his face. "Are you crazy? I'm not gettin' out of this car. That's how women get abducted or do ye no watch *CSI*?" Surreptitiously, she shoved the lock on the door with her thumb, fully aware that he could simply unlock it again by sticking his hand into her open window. Ridiculous, but she felt more secure anyway.

He crossed his arms over his chest, the tablet tucked under one elbow. "We got a call about you. Apparently, you've been driving on the wrong side of the road for several miles."

Had she? She thought for minute. Sweet Lord, she had! She closed her eyes, then opened them, deciding to give humor a try.

She beamed up at him. "Officer, I prefer to think of it as this whole country drives on the *wrong* side of the road—*I'm* drivin' on the right side of the road."

He tapped one finger against the biceps of the opposite arm and sighed deeply again. "I realize this is probably nothing more than you not paying attention to the rules of the road here in Indiana...well, in the whole United States, for that matter. But I won't be doing my official duty if I don't verify your sobriety. Particularly since you have a backseat full of wine. That's the reason I'm going to ask you to blow into a breathalyzer or walk a straight line for me." He bent down again and peered at her. "Your choice."

Kitt stared right back at him. "Am I allowed one phone call?"

LIEUTENANT RYKER LANGE couldn't remember when he'd enjoyed a traffic stop more, particularly since he hadn't made one in a while. First of all, Kathleen Eleanor Boynton was undoubtedly one of the most strikingly beautiful women he'd ever seen. And he'd seen a lot of very pretty women in his thirty-three years on the planet. A lot. Dark brown hair with reddish glints that glistened in the late-morning sun, creamy white and peach skin, a pert little nose sprinkled with freckles, and the bluest eyes he'd ever stared into. Sapphire blue. Sea blue. Blue like an Indiana October sky. As blue as…he ran out of apt comparisons as he pulled his attention back to her question.

He blinked. "A phone call?"

She nodded. "Aye."

When she said it, he didn't smell any alcohol on her breath, so that left out that part of probable cause, but there was still the matter of the cases of wine in the backseat and the recorked bottle nestled next to her purse on the floor. Yes, he had recognized Bren Flaherty's old Jeep Wrangler before he ever ran the plate or checked the registration. He was fairly certain she hadn't stolen it; no doubt this was some relative of the Flahertys who had borrowed Bren's car. However, this was getting fun. Besides, her clear Irish brogue charmed the heck out of him. "The phone call doesn't happen until *after* I arrest you."

She leaned one elbow on the bottom of the steering wheel and cupped the sweet but stubborn curve of her chin in her palm. "Are you planning on arresting me, then?"

"Only if you resist proving sobriety, Miss Boynton."

She rolled her eyes. "Oh, for the love of all that's holy. Move your arse." As she reached down, Rye's hand went automatically to the gun on his hip and he backed away. Kathleen snorted. "Don't shoot! I'm just openin' my door." She slid out of the car, both hands in the air in a gesture of surrender. "Now watch, 'cause I only intend to do this for ye one time. I'm late for a meeting and it's bloody cold out here."

When she rose from the seat, he nearly lost his breath. She was stunning—dressed in a pair of skinny jeans tucked into brown suede low-heeled ankle boots, a fleece-lined denim jacket over a tucked-in FOUR IRISH BROTHERS WINERY T-shirt, and a jaunty royal-blue knitted scarf around her neck. She was tall, five-foot-eight according to her driver's license, and curvy in all the right places, with legs that went on forever.

She strode over to a yellow line that demarcated a parking spot a few feet away, extended her arms, and placed one booted foot in front of the other. "Ye watchin', sir?"

He was watching all right. Those snug jeans displayed the cutest butt he'd seen in ages, and it swayed real nice as she balanced on the line like a tightrope walker. Gracefully, she took about fifteen steps, executed a perfect spin, and walked back toward him, her eyes locked with his.

When she got within a half-dozen feet of him, she stopped and crossed her arms over her high, full breasts and quirked one brow. "Satisfied?"

Hardly. He wanted to keep her here as long as possible, learn more about her. He tilted his head toward the Jeep. "Do you know what an open container law is, Miss Boynton?"

Her blue eyes widened. "No."

Leisurely, he shoved the stylus back into the side of the e-ticket machine, taking his time reattaching it to his wide leather belt, while Miss Kathleen Eleanor Boynton fidgeted with her long ponytail.

"In Indiana, you cannot possess an open bottle of alcohol in the passenger area of a car."

She frowned. "They're all in boxes. Besides, this car has no boot. I'm just deliverin' them to my cousin Sean down at the Four Irish Brothers Winery in town there." Her eyes narrowed, but not before he thought he read a hint of uneasiness in their blue depths. "Surely ye know the Flahertys."

He was making her nervous and although he rather enjoyed her discomfiture after her haughty display of temper, he didn't want her to be afraid of him. He just wanted to her to linger. "What about the bottle on the floor next to your purse?"

Her expression switched back to the self-confident smile she'd worn earlier. "That's not open. It's been recorked."

He leaned against the front fender of the Jeep. "Semantics."

She took the few steps to the car, pushed the door closed with that gorgeous behind, and leaned against it. The chill breeze blew a few dark tendrils of hair into her face and she raked it back with her fingers. "What's your name, officer? Do you have some ID?"

He laughed. "Do you mean other than the badge I'm wearing, the uniform, and the River's Edge Police Department automobile sitting right there?"

She scraped a wisp of hair away from her lips again. "Your name?"

Now they were getting somewhere. "Lieutenant Ryker Lange, miss." He held out the leather case that contained another badge and his official police department photo ID. He'd just made lieutenant a month ago and a swell of pride rose in his chest as he snapped open the new badge wallet.

Kathleen peered at it, tilting her head in an adorable manner. "And how often do you stop young women on the pretext of a traffic violation when, clearly, what you really want is to flirt with them?"

"I'm just maintaining law and order, miss."

"Right." She straightened. "Okay if I get back in?"

"Sure. Just keep your hands where I can see them."

Releasing a huge, dramatic sigh, she yanked open the door and slipped into the driver's seat. "I'm really running late. I'm sorry about driving in the wrong lane. 'Twas a mistake. In the future, I'll make every attempt to remember I'm no longer in Ireland, where we drive on the correct side of the road." She gave him a sunny smile. "What shall we do about the open container violation, then?" she asked, her tone conversational. "I'm going to reach down here and get it, aye?"

He nodded, too taken with her to wonder what she was

up to until she held the dark-green bottle out to him.

"Here, you take it." She shrugged. "I was going to have a glass with some cheese and biscuits while Sean and I had a meeting, but I don't want to be breaking the law when I've only been two weeks in your charming town."

"Are you offering me a bribe?"

She scoffed. "Hardly. I'm trying to get the damned thing out of my car."

Rye found it increasingly difficult to maintain his stern visage as he gazed at the beautiful woman holding the bottle of Four Irish Brothers Winery pinot noir out her car window. For the moment, he ignored her offer. "Just out of curiosity, what brings you to the US, Miss Boynton? A vacation? Visiting the Flahertys?"

The hostility in her eyes cooled slightly. "I'm visiting, helping out at their winery a bit."

She was thawing. Nice. He pursued his quest for information. "What are you doing for them?"

"I'm helping get some new marketing and events ideas going." Her expression shuttered just as quickly as it had opened. "They're no paying me if that's what worries ye. I've not got a work visa…yet. Do ye want to take this so I can be on my way or shall I toss it in that bin over there?" She jerked head toward the dumpster behind the post office.

Somehow, he managed to contain the delighted smile inside him at the word *yet*. Could that mean she might be staying in River's Edge? Instead, he walked the few paces from the front of her car, took the bottle from her, and went around to the back of the Jeep to open the window above the tailgate and spare tire. He tucked the wine down between two cases, making sure it was securely stowed and wouldn't tip over. Pulling the window back down, he latched it and then sauntered back to the driver's-side door.

Before he could speak, Kathleen chuckled and shook her head. "Well, that was kind of ye, sir. Tossin' even a drop of that wine would've been a crying shame." Then she looked up at him, her blue eyes sparkling. "Now what? May I be on my way?"

Taking a deep breath, he gave her the full force of the Ryker Lange smile. The one that had won hearts in River's Edge and surrounding towns since he was fifteen. "Well, Miss Kathleen Boynton—"

"Kitt."

"I'm sorry?"

"I'm called Kitt. Only my ma calls me Kathleen and then only if she's unhappy with me." She gave him a demure smile. "And you're not unhappy with me anymore, are you, Lieutenant Lange?"

"I-I..." Ryker's heart pounded as he stared into her eyes and got lost in the ocean-blue depths. With effort, he pulled his gaze away and looked out over the top of her car, swallowing hard to get his runaway thoughts into some semblance of order. She was doing to him exactly what he'd planned to do to her. *Yikes!*

Okay, Rye, get yourself together.

This was a simple traffic stop. *He* was a respected lieutenant on the River's Edge Police Department, not some high school freshman taken with the new girl in school. Although, truth be told, that was exactly how he felt, and it was a very unfamiliar sensation. He didn't like it one bit.

He cleared his throat. "Miss Boynton. I'm going to let you go with a verbal warning. But in the future, please pay attention and remember that you're driving in the United States now." He tapped the edge of the door frame. "You can go." Then he held up one hand. "Wait, if you plan on staying for a while, you might want to get an Indiana driver's license."

"I don't know what my plans are, but I've applied for an H1B visa. If I don't get the work visa, I shan't be worrying you for long. Soon enough, I'm back to Ireland and driving on the correct side of the road."

His joy at the news that her staying in River's Edge was a possibility disconcerted him so much he simply gave her a brief nod as he stepped away from the car. "Have a nice day."

She pulled her seat belt across her chest and the smile she gave him sent a zip of heat right through him. "You have a fine day, too, Lieutenant."

Never let it be said that love at first sight wasn't a real thing because, in that moment, Ryker Lange fell in love for the very first time in his life.

Chapter Two

"**H**EY, YOU OKAY?" Kitt's cousin Sean's expression was a study in worry as he loped out of the in-town tasting room toward the Jeep. He glanced at his smart watch. "I thought you were going to be here at eleven. I'm opening in thirty and we haven't had a chance to talk."

"Sorry, coz." Kitt slipped out the seat and ran around to meet Sean at the back of the car, where he was opening up the tailgate. "I got stopped by a guar—um, a policeman."

Sean halted mid-reach and turned around. "What? Why?"

Heat rose in her cheeks and she looked away from his piercing blue gaze. "I was drivin' on the wrong side of the road." She pulled a case of port out of the back of the car, then before it could tip over, quickly caught the recorked bottle of pinot that Lieutenant Lange had placed there. "And for having an open container in the passenger part of the car."

"Oh, I can't wait to hear *this* story." Sean picked up the bottle, set it on the case he was unloading, and with a chin hitch motioned her to go ahead of him into the building.

The door was propped open in spite of the chilly January air, so she carried her burden back to the tiny storeroom before heading back out for another. Once they got the Jeep unloaded, Kitt unwrapped her scarf and hung her jacket up, preparing to start on the task of filling the wine racks in the tasting room, but not before taking a deep breath as she stared out across the mighty Ohio River.

Lots of things about Indiana reminded her of Ireland, but this wide, meandering river was *not* one of them. The Ohio River was nothing at all like the controlled River Liffey, which ran through the heart of Dublin, the city built up on either side. She used to walk along the Liffey on her lunch hour to clear her head after long difficult meetings with clients at Walsh, McCarthy and O'Connor Advertising, the firm where she'd worked for nearly ten years.

The trees on the opposite shore in Kentucky were bare, their skeleton branches reaching toward the blue winter sky, while a coal barge made its way east on the water. Closer to the shore, a couple of bundled-up kayakers paddled along, and even though the sun was shining, Kitt shivered, wondering how they could stand the brisk breeze. She remembered her cousin Aidan's story at family supper the night before about how the Ohio had always been a highway of industry even before Indiana became a state. Fur trappers in canoes navigated its rapids and wide flatboats carried goods and pioneers in covered wagons westward. Her actor cousin told a dramatic story, and it made her excited to go down to the Falls of the Ohio state park to hear more about the river and its impact on Indiana and the rest of the Midwestern US.

There was so much to learn, particularly if she expected to stay, apply for dual citizenship one day, and not return to Ireland. At least not to live. Her throat closed up and she shook her head. No use thinking about that now. There were racks to fill and she needed to show Sean some of her ideas for winter and spring events and advertising at Four Irish Brothers Winery.

She took a deep breath, blinking back the tears as she began to load the bottles into the wooden racks along the wall. *Stop now. No regrets.* But that police officer reminded her too much of what she was running away from…or rather *whom*. It wasn't that he looked like Ethan. In fact, Sean resembled Ethan's dark good looks more closely than Ryker Lange did. No, it was his attitude—a self-assured, ever-so-slightly arrogant demeanor. An *I'm-sexy-and-I-know-it* kind of charm that had swept her off her feet the first time Ethan Craine had walked into the conference room at Walsh, McCarthy and O'Connor. She swiped at her cheek, furious with herself for allowing Ethan to even enter her mind.

The rat bastard.

The married *rat bastard!*

"Hey, labels up, coz." Sean grinned at her as he set another case of wine beside her.

Kitt shook her head. "Sorry." She spun the bottles she'd already placed before setting any new ones in the slots. "My mind is wandering."

"You okay?"

She yanked a tissue from her jacket pocket and blew her nose. "Cold makes my eyes water."

Thankfully, he didn't push it. Instead, Sean knelt beside her and opened a case of Riesling. "Want to tell me about being stopped? Who was it?"

Heat rose in her cheeks again as she thought about Ryker Lange. "It was a Lieutenant Lange."

Sean glanced at her. "Rye? He's a good guy. He usually doesn't do traffic stops anymore, though."

Actually, Ryker Lange had come across as rather cocky. However, she wasn't going to argue that point with her cousin because, honestly, she didn't trust her judgment about men anymore. Hadn't the last two years proved she had no discernment whatsoever? "He was very kind. I *was* driving on the wrong side of the road. I'm going to have to pay more attention." She swallowed hard. "I'm sorry, Sean. I'll get used to things here, I promise. And hopefully before I kill myself or someone else."

Sean patted her shoulder. "I know you will. I'm not worried about it. We'll stick a note to the dash in Jeep that says KEEP TO THE RIGHT. That's what I did when I drove in Ireland on vacation, except, of course, mine said KEEP TO THE LEFT."

Kitt sat back on her heels. "I felt like a bloody idiot. Then he saw that recorked bottle of pinot." She lifted her chin toward the bottle she'd set on the tasting bar. "What's the deal with open containers?"

Sean shrugged. "The law in Indiana. Conor should've told you to put it way in the back."

"Not his fault; he wasn't there. Bren loaded the car up at the winery and brought it to me at Conor's. I grabbed the bottle off the table before I left, thinkin' we could have it with our lunch. I'll know next time." She stacked a few more bottles, then turned to her cousin. "He thought I'd been drinkin'. He made me walk a straight line in a car park." She chuckled. "I guess I can't blame him for that, either, can I? After all, I *was* drivin' on the wrong side of the road."

"Did he ticket you?"

"No, no citation. Just a verbal warning."

"Well, that's good. A traffic citation for reckless driving wouldn't serve you while you're applying for your permanent work visa." He gazed at her, his blue eyes a mirror of her own, an eager expression on his handsome face. "That is, if you decide to stay here. I hope you do, Kitt. We need you and, I confess, all four us have loved hearing a real Irish brogue again."

She returned his smile and rose, picking up the case she'd just emptied. "Aye, well then, I guess I'll have to stay. After all, whatever the accent is here, it certainly doesn't sing like a brogue now, does it?"

"Nope." Sean stood, too, and stacked his empty case on top of hers. "Take these back and I'll go turn over the sign. We need to make sure we have some cheese and sausage trays made up. The sun's out, which means we'll get plenty of tourists in today and they're usually hungry."

As she took the case back to the storeroom, her thoughts again wandered back to the handsome police lieutenant. *Ryker Lange.* His smile had been killer and, at one time in her life, he would've charmed the socks right off her. Because *once*, she was open and ready to be charmed. Once. Before she stopped believing in fairy-tale endings and happily-ever-afters.

"Rye Lange *is* a nice guy." Sean's voice startled her, causing her to drop the last wine case divider she'd pulled out of a cardboard box.

She spun around, then with precision placed the divider on top of the pile she'd started. "I'm sure."

He lifted the stack of separators and dropped them all into an empty carton. "He's single."

She eyed him. "And I would care about that...why?"

Sean picked up the carton of cardboard dividers and headed for the door. "Just thought I'd mention it. That's all."

As Kitt followed him, she stuck her tongue out at his back in a childish gesture.

"I saw that," Sean said over his shoulder.

"Saw what?"

"You're reflected in the sliding glass doors, goofy." He talked as he walked, and she trailed behind him. "What's wrong with me offering a little information about Ryker Lange? That's all it was, just chitchat. Idle chitchat."

"What crap." She scooted around him in the car park and opened the boot...er, tailgate of the Jeep so he could shove the box inside. "We agreed up front you guys were *not* going to try to fix me up with anyone here. I told you I'm done with men. My judgment in that area sucks. I always fall for the worst possible person, thus, the rule is simple. No dates. Do ya remember that, coz?"

"I'm not fixing." Sean gave her a pointed look. "Simply,

you know…chatting."

"Well, you can stop, because I do not care to know anything at all about Ryker Lange." With a huff, she headed back into the tasting room, nearly crashing into a loaded rack of wine paraphernalia, bumping off several corkscrews and cards of wine rings. "Dammit." She picked up the scattered accessories, then stomped over to the glass refrigerator to gather the items to make cheese trays.

RYKER LEANED AGAINST the brand-new fire truck—a *quint*, according to his older brother, Becker, who had recently been named assistant fire chief for the town of River's Edge. He said the huge truck was a good choice for smaller departments because it combined five jobs, which offhand, Rye couldn't name. Beck sure seemed proud of the thing, though.

Beck tapped his shoulder as he passed by, a rag in his hand. "Don't lean on the machinery. I'm trying to get the water spots off of it."

Rye pulled away from the truck and moved to the pole nearby. "Is shining vehicles still part of your job description since you got promoted?"

Beck just stared at him. "I'm a firefighter. It's a part of every firefighter's job to take care of the equipment."

Rye raised both hands in surrender. His brother had been touchy as hell ever since he came home from Indy last year. It didn't take much to set him off and Rye wasn't interested in wrangling. He was there on a fishing expedition, looking for anything his dear older brother might know about the delectable Kitt Boynton. "Sorry. Hey, did you know the Flahertys have a cousin visiting from Ireland?"

"Nope."

"They do."

"Cool."

When Becker didn't add anything more, Rye tried again. "She's helping out with the winery."

"Okay." Beck continued rubbing, folding the rag over and starting on a new section of the truck.

"Have you seen her around town? Like at Mac's or the Tea Leaf?" Ryker gestured with an up-to-here hand above his shoulder, offering more of a description of the lovely Miss Boynton. "She's tall, long, dark reddish hair, incredible body."

"Nope."

"I pulled her over today."

Beck gave him a wry grin. "Are traffic stops still part of your job description since you got promoted to lieutenant?"

Rye chuckled. "Touché, brother. I'm still on the beat now and then by choice. I like to know what's going on around town and getting out among them is the only way. Back to the cousin—she was driving on the wrong side of the road. Forgot she was in the US."

Beck stopped polishing and crossed his arms over his chest, the rag dangling from his right hand. "Okay, clearly you're headed somewhere with this, so talk."

"I'm not headed anywhere," Ryker denied. "She's very

pretty, that's all. And she has an Irish accent. Man, it was cute."

Beck gazed at him for a moment, then sighed. "No, Rye. Don't."

"Don't what?"

"Do *not* go after her." He returned to his task. "She's the Flahertys' cousin. You mess with her and you'll have all four of them on you like ducks on a June bug, as Mom would say."

"I'm not going to *mess* with her. What does that even mean anyway?" Ryker shoved his hands into his jacket pockets and shifted uncomfortably against the cold metal support. "I just thought I'd ask her out. Maybe meet for a cup of coffee. She can accept or not."

"I thought you were dating that new front desk clerk at the Cotton Mill. What's her name?"

"You know her name is Tracy. You had dinner with us a couple of weeks ago. It was just a couple of dates…not a relationship. We decided we were better off as friends. I just thought you might know something about the cousin since you're friends with Bren and Tierney." Ryker had had exactly four dates with Tracy Knox. She was fun, but they'd both realized pretty quickly that it wasn't meant to be. He was glad they had ended it before they got too entangled.

"I haven't seen Bren in about a month—he's been out of the country. Just got back." Becker stooped next to the rear bumper. "How long has this cousin been here?"

"Just a couple of weeks, she said."

"Well, that's why I don't know anything about her"—he

straightened—"and even if I did, I wouldn't share it with you because you are a dirty dog when it comes to women, Rye." He said it with a teasing grin and a head shake, but still, it stung.

"Thanks a lot." Rye didn't bother denying the accusation because in his heart of hearts, he knew there was a grain of truth to it, although he didn't truly believe he ever offered any woman anything more than he was willing to give. As he got older, he'd realized that he simply enjoyed the company of women—didn't matter if they were short or tall, slender or curvy, young or old. He was just as inclined to tease Paula Meadows at the Bread and Butter Bakery when he stopped by for the free doughnut she offered all first responders each day as he was to flirt with Tracy Knox. He wasn't a dirty dog about it—at least he didn't think he was. Not like his father—*never* like that. He appreciated the attention, relished the back-and-forth, but he was never inappropriate with any woman. And he never made promises he had no intention of keeping. He *always* told the women he dated the truth.

"Just calling 'em as I see 'em. You go through women like most of us go through a bag of chips." Becker headed toward the firehouse kitchen, indicating with a head tilt for Rye to follow. "Want some chicken casserole? Just made it this morning."

Ryker wasn't sure he wanted to have a sit-down with his older brother at the moment. He was only on a lunch break and this was getting him nowhere anyway. Clearly, Beck knew nothing at all about Kitt Boynton. Besides, Rye was in no mood to deal with Beck's gloomy rambling about women and relationships and loves lost. "'Preciate the invite, bro, but I've got to get back to work." He turned to go out the service door next to the tall overhead at the front of the firehouse, when Becker's voice stopped him.

"Rye, seriously. Just *no* to the Flahertys' cousin, okay?"

Ryker grinned over his shoulder. "Whatever you say, Beck." He waggled his fingers over his head and walked out of the firehouse.

He slid into his squad car, turned the key, and waited for the engine to warm up. Kitt had said she was headed to the Flahertys' in-town tasting room. He glanced at his watch. Only about twenty-five more minutes before he needed to be back at the station. Buckling his seat belt, he turned the ignition key and pulled out of the firehouse parking lot, heading toward Riverview Road. Maybe he'd grab a takeout container of cheese, sausage, and crackers. He sure did love that Sycamore Hills smoked Gouda they sold there...and he hadn't had lunch yet.

A familiar frisson of excitement tingled through him as he approached the cedar-and-glass building that overlooked the river. It was the same adrenaline high he got when he played a great game of tennis or when he and his brother Max sped their wave runners across the choppy water of the river. The sensation intensified when he saw the Jeep parked at the far end of the lot. She was there.

Slowing the car, he signaled to turn, but suddenly, almost unconsciously, he flipped it off again and passed up the tasting room as Beck's words came back to him.

Do not go after her. You are a dirty dog when it comes to

women.

A mile east of the tasting room, he pulled into one of several scenic overlooks along the road and put the car in PARK. Frost gleamed on the shore and in the trees on the other side of the river.

Kitt's face, her dimpled smile, her blue, blue eyes, and her long dark hair appeared in his brain, the image of her walking the line in the parking lot, her butt swaying enticingly, and those legs. Those incredible long legs—pictures that had been looping in his head since she'd driven away from the traffic stop with a jaunty wave out her window. The clear intelligent look in her eyes and the easy way she put him in his place. He shoved his fingers through his carefully tousled hair. What the heck was the matter with him? He'd never hesitated to go after anything—or anyone—he wanted.

But this was different. *She* was different, and he was damned if he knew why. He blew out a long breath, put the car in gear, and turned around to head back to the station house. The high...that rush, that thrill he'd felt at the sight of her car had never *ever* occurred over the possible pursuit of a woman before today.

Maybe because before, he always knew he would win, and with Kitt Boynton, he wasn't so sure. All he knew for certain was that he wanted to know her...

Chapter Three

Kitt followed Carly Hayes up the wooden steps to the apartment above Graham "Mac" Mackenzie's garage, noting that even though Carly was about the same age as Ma, she certainly couldn't have been more different. Carly was tiny, delicate, and shapely, where Ma was tall, muscular, and comfortably round. Carly's brows were perfectly arched and her nails professionally manicured, while Ma barely had time to wash her face each day and her nails were frequently rough and broken from working with the horses. However, as the older woman reached the wooden landing at the top of the stairs and turned, the smile she offered sent a bolt of homesickness right through Kitt. For all that Sam Flaherty's ma may have looked like what Da would call a *fancy feek*, she was warm as the summer sun. Just like Ma.

Carly unlocked the apartment door and held out her hand. "Here you go. We scrubbed it from top to bottom and the furniture is basically a compilation of the stuff Meg didn't take when she married Sean and my things from Chicago, although I sold a lot of it when I made the move down here. The bed was mine, but the mattress is new and a lot of the stuff in the kitchen is from my house in Chicago. Aidan was the last person to live here." She chuckled. "We seem to be the landing spot for Flahertys who need a nest."

Kitt's jaw dropped at the charming scene before her—an inviting deep sofa with soft denim slipcovers, a wing chair and ottoman, even a tall entertainment center with a flat-screen TV and several other pieces of equipment, including a Blu-ray player. She would definitely have Maeve send her the DVDs of the horse shows and copies of other recorded family events. They would help with the homesickness. A small dining area separated the lounge from a decent-sized kitchen, while a hallway opposite the front door led to a rather large bedroom and a bathroom that backed up to the kitchen.

Trailing down the hall after Carly, Kitt smiled when Sam's mother offered a rather deprecating smile. "No tub, sorry. A pretty good-sized shower, though. Graham and I have a hot tub down on the deck that you're welcome to use anytime you like. We keep it on all year 'round. I'll show you how to turn it on if you decide you want the place."

Kitt's curiosity clamored for more details about this woman, whose silver-threaded auburn hair was pulled into a messy bun atop her head and whose deep brown eyes sparkled with obvious joy at the mere mention of the handsome diner owner's name. Oddly, in spite of her lack of makeup, the snug jeans, the RIVERSIDE DINER T-shirt she wore, and the unmistakable odor of frying bacon wafting around her, she was the most elegant creature Kitt had ever met. "When did you leave Chicago?"

Carly straightened the spring-green towels on the rack by the shower and peeked into the stall as if verifying that all was well behind the flowered curtain. "About three years ago. Not long after Sam and Conor got married. I came down for the wedding, learned to know my daughter again, and fell in love with the town." She blushed prettily. "And with Graham."

Kitt couldn't help smiling. Dear Lord, was everyone in this town crazy in love? It was almost enough to make her believe in the *magic of River's Edge* that Bren and Aidan talked about endlessly. But her wiser nature immediately smacked her. Love made you foolish. Wasn't she a living testament to that? *Crazy* in love was the stuff of fairy tales and films—it wasn't real life. "Everyone else calls him Mac. Why do you call him Graham?"

Carly smiled and shrugged. "It's his name and I like it, plus it's a way to show him how I feel without getting sappy in public." She rubbed her palms together as they returned to the front door. "Want to walk back to the diner with me? I think the special tonight is roasted chicken with new red potatoes and poached asparagus. Paula brought French silk pie today and there might be some left. Supper's on me and you can sign the lease with Graham." She closed the door and locked the dead bolt above the keypad handle before holding up the keychain. "That is, if you like the apartment."

Kitt chuckled. "I *adore* the apartment. It's exactly what I want and I'm awfully glad Mr. Mackenzie is willing to do a month-by-month lease. And let *me* buy supper tonight, okay?"

Carly nodded and handed her the key. "He'll need a check for two months' rent when you sign the lease, prorated and refundable if you leave before then. The regular rent payment is due on the fifteenth of each month. You can drop it off down at the house or to one of us at the diner or give it to Meg, if you like. She does all the books for Graham. Is that okay?"

A rush of pleasure washed over Kitt. "Better than okay." *My own place! In America!* She couldn't wait to sign the lease and move in the few things she'd brought with her from Ireland. Once her visa came through, she'd have Maeve ship her the four boxes of books, clothes, and other personal items that were packed and waiting in the Dublin apartment she'd sublet to her sister and her new husband, Declan. This charming apartment was nothing at all like the one she'd left, which overlooked the Liffey from the fifth floor of a modern building on Sir John Rogerson's Quay.

She stood at the back door of Mac and Carly's brick house while Carly ran inside for the paperwork. Thank the Lord that the little garage apartment *was* so different from her uber-modern apartment in Dublin. It would be easier to banish all the memories of nights spent with Ethan. Or more often, sitting on the balcony with a glass of Jameson, watching the people below meandering along the river, while she wondered where Ethan was, what he was doing. That was before she'd learned he was a bastard and a liar. Before that awful evening when she'd encountered him—*and his fami-*

ly—at Killkenney Café, where she'd stopped for a quick bite with a classmate from grad school.

The image was imprinted on her brain, and no amount of crying or anger or cantering Dewey across a field or chocolate or Jameson could erase it. The merest thing could bring it forward—a svelte blonde woman passing her on the street in Temple Bar, a mother pushing giggling children in a pram, a family around a table in the window of a restaurant. There it would be, rushing into her head—Ethan sharing a meal with his wife and two daughters, his dark head thrown back as he laughed at something his wife had said, his hand touching her shoulder with such clear affection.

As soon as she realized it was him and who he was with, Kitt had tucked into a corner of the café, fumbling with her purse, and wrapping her scarf high around her neck, trying to simply disappear into the woodwork. Caroline, who was taking the graduate internet marketing class with her at Trinity College, had eyed her curiously. "Kitt, what's wrong? You look as if you've seen a ghost."

Trembling, Kitt had pushed away from the small round table. "I've got to get out of here."

Carrie gathered up the sandwiches and crisps they had just spread out before them and shoved them into her bag. Later, Carrie would tell her that she'd turned white as a sheet, but her friend still toasted her moxie when Kitt marched up to the happy family.

It took all she had inside her not to scream at him, not to smack him across the face, or toss his beverage in his lap. Instead, calmly, she'd greeted him formally, "Why, Mr.

Craine. Hello."

Speaking of turning white as a sheet, the color had drained from Ethan's face as soon as he saw her standing behind his little girls. For a moment, he simply sat, jaw dropped. He recovered with panache, she had to give him that. "Hullo, Ms. Boynton. Darling, this is Kathleen Boynton, one of the marketing directors at work." He rose and extended a hand toward the others at his table. "This is my wife, Phoebe, and our daughters, Melanie and Annabelle." He cleared his throat, a look of clear desperation in his eyes. "What brings you to Trinity this time of night?"

He knew perfectly well that she was taking a class. They'd talked about it only the night before as they lay on her bed in a rumple of sheets. With all her heart, Kitt had wished one could kill with just a look, because Ethan Craine would've been flat out on the floor, bleeding from the heart. Carrie had rescued her from any further conversation, hurrying her out of the café and down the street before stopping at a bench near the river, where Kitt had sat trembling and too shaken to even cry.

Carly's voice behind Kitt startled her out of the bad place. "Okay, got everything I need. Let's go get some supper."

"Love to." Kitt linked arms with the older woman and they headed for Mac's Riverside Diner. She shoved Ethan Craine into a dark cobwebby corner of her conscious mind, hopefully for good this time.

"HERE YOU GO, Rye." Mac set a platter in front of him and Ryker inhaled the delicious aroma of Mac's amazing turkey burger and a side of sweet potato fries with roasted garlic aioli. Mac added a small dish of slaw. "Slaw's on me. It's a new dressing recipe. Tell me what you think."

Rye grinned. "Yours or Carly's?" The whole town knew Mac had been letting Carly experiment in his kitchen, a rarity afforded to very few. Well, no one really, except Carly.

"Hers. Be honest, though, because I thought it was an odd combination and she wouldn't share the whole recipe with me. Kicked me out of the kitchen while she mixed it up this morning. You're the first guinea pig." Mac went back into the kitchen, returning immediately to the counter where Ryker sat, carrying a small cup and another fork. "Here, we'll taste it together before she gets here. If it sucks, I'll break it to her tonight after I close."

Rye took a bite of slaw, letting the flavors sit on his tongue for a moment. He didn't consider himself particularly a gourmet, but he always enjoyed Mac's food. Hell, he enjoyed any food he didn't have to cook himself. Most of the restaurant and café owners in town had learned his favorites over the years; he barely had to look at a menu wherever he went. "I taste mustard and is it...oh, damn!" He swallowed and then sipped from his water glass. "That's hot sauce, isn't it?"

Mac nodded as he took another bite of the shredded cabbage salad. "Little bit of hot sauce, yeah. Sugar and vinegar..."

Rye tried another forkful, prepared this time for the spicy

flavor. It was actually pretty good. "Celery seed, red onion. Hmmm...I think she's got a winner here, Mac." He opened his bun and spread a bit of the slaw on his turkey burger before taking a big bite. "Really good on the burger, too."

Mac scraped out the last of the slaw and popped it in his mouth. "She did it. We're adding her mustard slaw to the menu. She'll be pumped. It's her first original dish."

Rye dipped a fry in the aioli. "Well, tell her I said good job. I'll definitely order it next time I'm in."

Mac set his dish in the sink behind him, turned, and gave Rye an over-the-glasses look. "So tomorrow, then?"

Rye just shrugged, not one bit offended. He ate at the Riverside a lot and made no apologies for it. "Probably."

"She'll be here in a few; you can tell her yourself. You'll make her day." Mac stepped down to the cash register to settle a check with Noah Barker, who'd come in with Dot Higgins for the third time in less than two weeks, by Rye's count.

He watched as Dot waited shyly by the door while Noah paid the bill. Something was definitely brewing there. Noah had been a widower for several years and Dot was what was once referred to as a *spinster*, although town lore had it that she'd suffered a broken heart many years earlier. Noah's hardware store was right down from Dot and her sister Mary's Seams Pieceful quilt store, and he had seen Noah making the trek between the two places more than once lately. Rye caught Dot's eye and winked. "You and Noah courting now, Dot? You aiming to break my heart?"

"Just you never mind, Ryker Lange." Dot shook one finger at him, but kept her position by the door. "Besides, we both know you could never keep up with me. I need a man with experience."

Noah's big laugh filled the diner, turning the heads of the other patrons. "She's gotcha there, Rye."

Rye chuckled. "She sure does." He waved as Noah opened the door. "Enjoy your evening, you two."

While he was turned around, he noticed a couple of women crossing the street in the crisp evening dusk.

Hold on. Is that Kathleen Boynton, heading straight for the diner with Carly?

His heart skipped a beat or two as the bell above the door jangled and the two women entered, chattering like old friends.

He spun back around on the stool, trying to be unobtrusive and not appear like he was gawking. Instead, he knocked over his glass of iced tea, the ketchup bottle, and the salt-shaker with his elbow. The tea spilled all over the counter and the ketchup and salt clattered to the floor behind the counter as heat rushed to his cheeks. "Oh, damn, I mean, darn, I mean..." Rye jumped up as iced tea ran off the counter onto his jeans. "No, no..." He grabbed a fistful of napkins from the dispenser on the counter and ended up knocking it off, too. "Crap..."

When he glanced up, Carly and Kitt were both obviously holding back laughter and a quick side-eye to Mac showed that he wasn't making any secret of a grin as he gathered up the fallen items beneath the counter. Mac tossed a dry towel and Rye caught it midair, applied it first to the front of his pants, and then started mopping up the stool and the red Formica counter.

Carly sauntered closer. "Um, could you use a little help there, Rye?" She opened the gate and joined Mac behind the counter.

Rye's cheeks continued to burn. "Thanks, Carly." He swiped ineffectually at his pants again. "Having a putz day, I guess."

Mac merely raised one brow as he wiped sweet tea off the ketchup bottle and placed it back with the rest of the condiments. Carly picked up the rogue napkin holder, which had somehow scooted far enough it hadn't landed in the puddle of tea, and set it next to the ketchup. The saltshaker was going to need some work, though. It made a wet ring when Mac set it back on the counter.

Kitt hurried over and grabbed it. "Quick, hold out your hand."

Rye couldn't imagine what she was doing. "What?"

"Hold out your right hand, palm up," she insisted, jiggling the saltshaker.

Mystified, Rye obeyed and she shook a few grains into his hand. "Quick now, toss that over your left shoulder."

"Um...okay." Rye furrowed his brows and released the salt over his left shoulder, then brushed his palms together. "What's that about?"

Kitt picked up the towel he'd set on the counter and began wiping down his stool and the one next to it. "It keeps the devil away."

"Sure, it does." Rye met Mac's gaze over the mess Carly

was busy mopping up on the counter. Mac merely raised one salt-and-pepper brow.

Kitt straightened up and handed the towel to Mac. "He's just there, you know, over your left shoulder…waitin'."

Rye glanced ruefully at his damp pants, deciding the embarrassment was a done deal, so he might as well follow along with this intriguing conversation. The brogue alone was enough to set his head spinning. "Is he now?" He sat back down.

Kitt perched on the stool next to him, her denim-clad knee brushing his as she turned slightly to face him. "Aye. And it's bad luck to spill salt, always has been. That kind o' carelessness invites the devil in."

"Really? Why?" The chatter in the diner had quieted. It seemed the rest of the patrons were as curious as he was.

Kitt's expression clearly told him she was stunned at his lack of knowledge on the topic of salt and the devil. "Of course, *really*. For many years, salt was hard to get and thus, quite precious; it was often used as currency way back in the old days. If you spilled it, you were invitin' bad luck or the devil into your life. But"—she held up one finger—"if you toss a few grains over your left shoulder after you spill salt, it gets in the devil's eyes and blinds him. Then he's powerless." She glanced around, suddenly aware that she'd become the center of attention. Color rose to her cheeks. "Um…at least that's what my ma always told me."

The small group of patrons burst into spontaneous applause and she offered a small nod before swinging her stool back around to face Carly and Mac. "Sorry," she whispered.

"Didn't mean to make a scene."

Mac grinned and Rye watched Kitt get drawn into the chef's magic, just like every other woman who walked into the diner. "No! That's a great story!" Mac extended a damp hand, then pulled it back. "Oops, sorry." He swiped it on his apron and put it out again. "Welcome back to the Riverside. Always glad to see you."

Once again, Kitt blushed and her smile lit up the room as she shook hands. "Good to see you, too. Looks like you're going to be my landlord."

Mac chuckled. "You like the apartment?"

Kitt nodded, her whole attention narrowed to the handsome diner owner. "Aye. It's lovely and thanks for doing a month-to-month lease. When may I move in?"

"Anytime you like. Tonight? Tomorrow?"

To Rye's ear, Mac's voice had dropped to a lower, more evocative timbre, which sort of made Rye want to grab him by his apron and remind him in no uncertain terms that his own lady was standing right in the kitchen with hot tongs in her hand. But when he glanced at Carly, she was smiling a warm, welcoming smile, clearly undisturbed by Mac's effect on females.

Rye fought the urge to spin Kitt's stool around so she faced *him* again. What the hell was the matter with him? He'd watched Mac Mackenzie turn on the charm with every woman who entered his door, even knew him to turn a grouchy male customer around with that million-dollar smile. Why did its effect on Kathleen Boynton make his stomach roil?

He took a deep breath and dove in. "You're renting Mac's garage apartment?"

Kitt tossed him a smile with a fraction of the wattage she'd given Mac just two minutes earlier. "I am."

"Well, that's great!" His voice was too hearty, so he toned it down a bit. "I mean, it's a nice place."

She nodded. "It is." She couldn't have seemed less interested in him if he'd been a fly on the wall, and when Carly came back from the kitchen with two steaming plates, Kitt rose from her stool and followed her to a booth across the room without so much as a glance at Rye.

Dammit, he was striking out. He eyed her over his shoulder, debating his next move when Mac sidled up to the counter.

"Dude, I'd think twice about going over there with the front of your pants all wet. Just sayin'."

Mac was right, but it sure seemed like an opportunity missed. One more peek over his shoulder showed him Kathleen Boynton was deeply engrossed in a conversation with Carly, and not paying one moment of attention to him. With a sigh, he tugged his wallet out of his pocket, tossed a tip on the counter, and side-walked to the register, where Mac waited, a barely contained grin on his face.

Rye handed him a twenty. "Any chance you'd let me sneak out the back? I really don't want to do a wet-pants walk of shame to the front door."

Mac chuckled softly and tilted his head toward the swinging gate behind the register. "Sure. Come on around."

Rye slipped behind Mac and hurried to the kitchen, then

out the alley door into the cold January evening with a head full of Kitt Boynton's Irish brogue and that fairy tale about the devil. A little smile formed on his lips as he remembered that Mac's garage apartment was a mere three blocks from his own cottage on Cedar Cliff Road, and he'd pass it every time he walked to town.

Chapter Four

KITT STACKED THE last of the valentine-making supplies on a long table at Four Irish Brothers Winery before once again checking the baskets of crafting materials to confirm they would have plenty.

"I can't believe you have a huge waiting list for this event!" Conor stepped out of the office and sauntered over to examine the red-checked ribbons, construction paper, card stock, paper lace doilies, candy hearts, and other valentine-y items laid out there. "People are actually paying us forty bucks a person just to come in and make a couple of fancy valentines, drink a glass of wine, and eat some snacks."

"It's all in how you present it. Plus, it's the middle of January. Holidays are over and folks are bored with winter." Kitt gave him a smile as she pulled pink, red, and white silk flowers from a bag, cut labels off, and set them in a basket. "If you want to help out here, you can start taking the tape off those spools of ribbon and then hang them on the rod in that box there."

Conor eyed the ribbon container she'd created out of a cut-down wine box and a dowel rod. "That's ingenious.

How much did all this stuff cost?"

"Well, most of it came from huge sales at about six craft and fabric stores in Cincinnati. Some it came from Holly's stash of Valentine's Day stuff that she was clearing out at the café, and some of this older stuff, like the lace and little Victorian postcards and old-fashioned valentines, are from some boxes that Judge Evans donated to the cause while he and Sam were cleaning out the attic at their law office. So, our cost was extremely low. Plus, this comes out of the advertising and promotion budget, which you guys have hardly touched yet this year."

Conor picked up a spool of red wired ribbon and scraped the tab off the end. "Well, pizza-and-wine nights all summer didn't need much promotion. They're a *thing* around here, and the Southern Indiana Wine Trail brochure was paid out of last year's budget, as were the giveaway glasses for the trail."

Kitt tossed another daisy in the basket. "We filled tonight's Pink Wine and Valentines with the first forty people who signed up and at last count, another thirty-two are on a wait list. I hated having to wait-list folks, but I didn't want to change the venue to someplace that would hold more people. This is about the winery."

Conor's brow furrowed in concentration. "Everyone gets snacks and one glass of our new rosé, but if they want more? They have to buy it, right?"

Kitt nodded. "They will...buy another glass, I mean. And bottles to take home." She tore open a bag of candy hearts and poured them into a bowl. "It's also about the fellowship, though, and having fun making pop-up cards and coming away with something pretty and romantic for Valentine's Day."

Conor started on another spool of ribbon. "I get it. We've always tried to emphasize the fellowship element of wine with everything we do here, so I'm really glad you're getting in the spirit, plus this is the perfect way to introduce the new rosé. Do we know who's coming tonight?"

Kitt lifted her chin toward the end of the table. "I just printed out the list that my events app created from the folks who signed up, but I haven't looked at it. Not that the names will mean much to me since I don't know too many people in town yet."

He wandered to the other end of the table and picked up Kitt's clipboard. "There's an app for that?"

She chuckled. "There's an app for everything, coz." The basket of silk flowers overflowed, so she grabbed another basket from under the table and began filling it. "I hung some flyers around town with your website on them so people could go online to sign up. Plus Facebook and Twitter. It worked."

"We have a Twitter account?"

Kitt laughed at Conor's blank expression. "We do now, and Instagram, too. I sent you all an email with links to our accounts."

"You put us on Instagram?"

"Yup. We have to be everywhere. It's how we do advertising these days. I'm seriously considering pricing out a Spotify or Pandora ad for the March Winemaker's Table we're having. I want to check that with you guys first."

"Winemaker's Table—I still can't get over that idea—wine and food with Mac. That's going to be the best. And what a great way to do something fun during a cold, gray month." Conor stepped back over to grab Kitt in a giant bear hug and swung her around. "Coz, do whatever you like. You are exactly what we needed here! None of us have a clue about marketing and advertising. We've always depended on word of mouth or the wine trail. You are going to make Four Irish Brothers Winery a household name all over the Midwest."

Kitt nearly dropped the flowers she'd been holding. "Put me down, you nutter! There's so much more we can do to bring the winery to a new generation of wine drinkers. Ya know, the median age of wine drinkers is going up, and we need to find ways to appeal to millennials, who are drinking spirits and beer more than wine. I think events, even things for families, may be a way to bring in a younger clientele."

Conor set her down, but not before dropping a quick kiss on her cheek. "I wish we could put you on the payroll."

"Well, ye canna, not until my work visa comes through. But I do appreciate your offer to pick up my rent. It wasn't necessary. I have plenty of savings to see me through 'til I decide what to do."

He brushed off her gratitude with a flip of his hand. "Small stuff. We gotta do something to compensate you for all your efforts."

The front door opened just then and Sean sauntered in on a blast of chill January air. "Wow! Love has arrived! Look at all this stuff." He fingered a length of ribbon before walking around the whole supply table, picking up a bit of lace here and a small felt heart there. "What can I do to help?"

"Sean-o, we're on Instagram and Twitter now!" Conor pulled out his phone. "I don't even have those on my phone yet. I barely have time to check Facebook once or twice a week."

Sean held up his cell phone. "I just started following us on both last night. Nice work, Kitt! The cover photos of the vineyard are amazing. Did you take those?"

Kitt nodded as she started putting together a pop-up valentine to use as a sample for her workshop participants. "From Bren and Tierney's porches. The one with the frosty trees and the river in the background was great, don't you think? I used it on our Facebook page, too."

Conor picked up the clipboard he'd abandoned in his enthusiasm and started reading off the names of the folks who'd signed up, when suddenly he stopped.

When she looked up from her task, he was holding the clipboard out to Sean and pointing to a name on it. Sean smirked and shook his head before eyeing Kitt with a grin.

"What?" she asked, halting in the middle of cutting strings of hearts out of red construction paper.

Sean raised one dark brow. "Seems you've got quite an...um, *eclectic* group here."

"Really?" Kitt set the card down. "Who's coming?"

Sean read from the list. "Well, Dot and Mary and Noah because wherever Dot goes, Noah's not far behind."

"We have a man signed up? That's wonderful!" Kitt never imagined the workshop would draw any men at all. These types of events were generally the exclusive territory of women.

"You've got men all right." Sean cleared his throat and finished reading the list Conor had started. Including Noah, eight of the names were men and when he read the last two names on the list, Kitt's heart began to beat faster. "Ryker Lange and Jane Lange."

Sean grinned and winked. "Looks like Lieutenant Lange is getting into the spirit of St. Valentine."

Kitt ignored the tacky inference, kept her eyes on her project, and casually asked, "Who is Jane Lange? Um…sister?" She avoided Sean's eyes. "Wife?"

Conor brought the list over and laid it down on the table next to Kitt. "That's his mom. She's a nurse at St. Mark's hospital in town. He's also got two brothers, Max and Becker. Max is an ER doc at St. Mark's. Beck is assistant fire chief."

Sean raised one dark brow. "I told you already Rye was single."

He'd caught her out. Pretending she didn't give a damn about Ryker Lange wasn't working, but Kitt managed to keep her tone indifferent. "Oh yeah, I forgot. A whole family of first responders, eh? Just like the O'Malley brothers back home." Too aware of the heat in her cheeks, she glanced down at the list. "Who are the other men on the list?"

Conor snickered and read over her shoulder. "Except for Mac and Noah Barker, who's dating Dot Higgins, every last one of them is single. Chaz LaGrotte is the day manager from the Cotton Mill Inn, Cameron and Joey Walker, two brothers from Walker Construction, Cary Eliot is a lineman for IKEC, Andy Shea is from the tire store up on the highway, and, hey, Sean, this is interesting—your old buddy from PT, Bobby Keller."

"*Bobby* signed up to make a valentine?" Sean's tone dripped disbelief.

Conor nodded. "I'd say the single guys in town are anxious to get a look at our Kitt here." He and Sean gazed at her with affection.

Kitt shook her head. "You two are eejits." She set the clipboard aside and continued working on the card she'd been creating. "It's entirely possible they're simply bored and looking for something different to do on a cold January night." She tossed them a defiant look. "Or maybe they're trying to impress some of the single women who've signed up."

Sean grabbed the clipboard and carried it to the tasting bar while Conor emptied cases of traminette, rosé, and gewürztraminer into the chiller by the door. "Um, I only see a few single gals on this list, kiddo. It's mostly moms looking for a night out and a couple of grandma types."

Kitt glared at him. "Seriously? You *know* everybody on that list?"

"Pretty much." Sean shrugged. "We've lived here all our lives and we own a popular business, so…" He lifted the page and started reading the names on the wait list. "But some of *these* names I don't recognize. This is going to be a terrific event, Kitt."

Conor grinned as he stashed the last of the bottles in the chiller. "And who knows? Maybe the man of your dreams will walk through the door ready to make a valentine and then sweep you off your feet."

Kitt merely scowled and shook her finger in the men's direction. "I'm no lookin' fer a man, dear cousins, dreamy or otherwise. Hop off that wagon right this minute and don't be getting' back on it, you hear?"

"RYE, HONEY, WHAT do you think?" His mom nudged his arm, nearly knocking his chin off his palm as he sat staring at Kathleen Boynton while she moved confidently from table to table. Black leggings and a lean red tunic covered in tiny white hearts made her appear svelte and sexy. Her dark hair, held off her face with a red scarf, streamed down her back and gleamed in the overhead lights. It looked so touchable, he was grateful his hands were busy with the valentine project.

"Rye!" Jane nudged him a little harder.

"*What*, Mom?" He turned toward her, immediately contrite at the sharpness in his tone. "I'm sorry, I was distracted." He focused on the pink paper valentine she was holding up, smiling when she opened it and a little teddy bear cutout popped up. "That's great. You mastered it."

"Harrumph." Jane looked at him over the top of her reading glasses. "Distracted indeed. Let's see yours."

For the hundredth time in less than two hours, Rye wondered what the hell he was doing at a stupid Pink Wine and Valentines party. First of all, he didn't drink—not beer, not liquor, and not wine, pink or otherwise. Second, he didn't have anyone to give a damn homemade valentine to, although his looked pretty good with different-sized hearts popping out in bouquet when he opened it for his mother's approval. He'd enjoyed chatting with Carly and Mac and surprisingly, even got a small kick out of making the pop-up card. But his attention had been divided all evening between his tablemates, his project, and their charming hostess.

Jane patted his hand. "That's adorable. Who's it for?"

He snorted a laugh. "I'd say it's probably going to be for you, Mom. You are my first and truest love."

Jane grinned. "You are so full of it, my son."

Rye's eyes wandered back to Kitt, who was deftly side-stepping Andy Shea's hand on her butt as she helped Harley Cole accordion-fold a strip of card stock. Rye's fingers curled into fists and he quickly dropped his hands into his lap. Shea had a lot of damn nerve, sitting there with sweet Harley, whom Rye had heard he was dating, yet playing grab-ass with Kitt.

As he gazed around the big, high-ceilinged room, his blood pressure rose another point or two. Bobby Keller had his hand in the air, looking for help with his project and so did Cary Eliot. In fact, what was up with all the single guys at what was clearly a girly event? Cary, Bobby, Cameron, and Joey all sat together at one table and hadn't stopped trying to attract Kitt's attention since she'd poured their first glasses of wine. The event seemed to have brought out a good number of the single wolves in town. Bobby Keller was physical therapist at St. Mark's and a good friend of Rye's brother Max. The guy had always rubbed Rye the wrong way, even way back in high school. Bobby had had it all—money, athletic ability, top grades, girls, and a cocky attitude that made Rye want to backhand him. That part hadn't changed since freshman year.

He craned his neck, searching for empty bottles on their table, but saw only the glasses they'd started the evening with as well as empty paper plates and napkins. *Damn.* No way to get them out of the place on a drunk-and-disorderly. They were raucous, teasing Kitt and catcalling like a bunch of college-aged idiots, but they weren't even buzzed.

When he looked back around, Kitt had disappeared from view.

"That's a nice one, Rye." A quiet voice behind his chair made him turn, but it was Holly Flaherty, not Kitt, who was admiring his handiwork.

He smiled up at her. "Thanks, Holly."

She picked it up and opened it, her smile growing at the bouquet of hearts that exploded from the inside. "Who's it for?"

Turning on the charm was pure instinct. "Haven't decided yet. Any chance I could convince you to dump that punk actor of yours and be *my* valentine? This remarkable card could be yours."

Holly chuckled and patted his shoulder. "Not a chance, Rye. Sorry. Besides, I don't think *I'm* the one you're interested in anyway." She leaned around to peer into his face before following his gaze to Kitt, who had reappeared and was laughing with Noah, Dot, and Mary while Chaz LaGrotte leered at her shapely behind from two tables away.

Holly trotted back to the bar while Mac laughed. "Yeah, if looks could kill, Chaz would be a goner."

Carly smiled. "All these single guys showing up sorta cramped your style tonight, didn't they, Rye?"

Heat crept up Rye's neck and into his cheeks. Dammit, was he so obvious? That Irish lass was putting him off his game and that was not good. Not good at all. Clearing his throat, he picked up a marker and added some subtle shading to the letters on the front of his valentine. "I have no idea what you're talking about. I'm here with my favorite girl." He winked at his mom, who simply gave him a knowing smile.

THE EVENT HAD nearly emptied out when Kitt slipped behind the tasting bar and nudged Holly, who was ringing up a bottle of vignoles for nursery school teacher Harley Cole. She couldn't hide the chortle of pleasure another moment. Her Pink Wine and Valentines event had turned out to be a huge success. "Wow, Holly. Everyone seemed to have a great time, enjoyin' themselves, drinkin' a bit o' wine, creatin' cards. It's officially been over for almost thirty minutes and there's still some folks lingerin'."

Holly finished ringing up the wine, had Harley sign the

point-of-sale tablet with her finger, and bagged the bottle. "We've sold quite a bit, too. However, that table over there"—she lifted her chin toward a raucous quartet of women near the big stone fireplace—"are on their third bottle since the free glass apiece we poured at the beginning, which by my count, means the four of them have had at least three, possibly four glasses each."

Kitt furrowed her brow. "The way they're getting louder and louder tells me they're feelin' no pain. They all came in together; however, they don't appear to have a designated driver. So what do we do?"

Holly began shoving corks back into the open bottles behind the bar. "Tonight, Aidan, Sean, and Bren are supposed to be the designated drivers, if need be. I don't see any of them at the moment."

"I think they all went downstairs to get cases to restock the racks." Kitt tapped her nails on the granite counter behind the bar. "I believe I'll wander over to that table with a tray of cheese and crackers and encourage them to nibble a bit until the guys get back up here."

"Good idea." Holly pulled a basket of dirty wineglasses from below the counter to take back to the dishwasher behind the office. "While you're about it, toss Ryker Lange a bone. He's been following your every move with those sexy bedroom eyes of his all night long."

Kitt reined in the urge to turn her head toward the table near the door where Ryker Lange, his mom, Mac, and Carly all sat admiring their valentines and chatting. That officer was a looker, no question about it, and she wasn't the only who'd noticed. The four women from the happy table had sidled past Ryker several times during the workshop as they'd collected supplies for their valentines. In spite of Holly's declaration that he'd been watching Kitt all evening, he'd flirted shamelessly with most of the women who'd attended.

Not that she was paying attention.

Who was she trying to kid? Of course she'd paid attention. He was delectable.

When Kitt cast a glance his direction, though, sure enough, he was watching her. She stepped around the tasting bar to take another tray of cheese and crackers to the rowdy girls, as she'd begun to think of them, and he rose to head her off.

"Evening, Kitt." His voice was like cream and just those two words sent a shiver through her.

She ignored the shiver, but stopped anyway. "Hullo, Lieutenant. I'm surprised to see you here."

His gray eyes turned a shade darker and his smile showed the most perfect teeth she'd ever seen. "Surprised, yet happy, right?"

She looked askance. "Well, we're always happy to see payin' customers here at Four Irish Brothers. Surprised because this event doesn't really seem like your kind of thing."

The blue sweater he wore made his brawny chest seem even broader...again, not that she was really paying attention, but he'd moved in another step closer. So close she caught the woodsy scent of his soap. "Oh, Irish, I'm as much of a fan of Valentine's Day as the rest of the folks here. Just wait until February fourteenth. The whole town looks like somebody dropped a net full of sappy on it. Not a single building escapes pink-and-white twinkle lights and heart-shaped garland. You'll see me out there with everyone else, festooning the streets with candy, romance, and flowers."

Kitt smiled up into his too-handsome face. "Festooning, eh? Well, good then. Delighted you enjoyed yourself." She stepped deftly around him and scurried over to the rowdy girls with the tray of nibbles before he got more charming and she got less resistant.

"Ladies, I thought ye might want a bit more to nibble on." She set the cheese and crackers in the center of the table and collected two empty wine bottles.

The blonde held up her card, which had turned out truly beautiful with red gingham ribbon, tissue paper hearts, and lace. "What do you think?"

"Not a bad job for being three sheets to the wind, Car-ol," one of the other women cackled. "Mine looks like my three-year-old did it."

Kitt glanced down and, honestly, couldn't argue the point—her card was pretty pitiful.

The way the other two chortled at the bedraggled attempt made Kitt decide they definitely had not appointed a designated driver. Glancing over her shoulder, she didn't see any of her Flaherty cousins close by. "Did you ladies come together tonight? Which one of you is the designated driver?" Kitt smiled as she asked the questions, even though she already knew the answers.

The blonde tittered and pointed. "We did. Mari is our

DD, aren't you, Mari?"

Mari, a short, round brunette who appeared to be a tad older than the others, chugged down the last of the wine in her glass before pulling her car keys out of her jeans pocket and jangling them at Kitt. "Yup, it's me." When she blinked, her pupils were awfully small, and she tilted slightly as she tipped back in her chair. Kitt's stomach dropped to her socks.

She glanced around for Bren, who was nowhere to be seen. However, Sean and Conor had explained to her when she'd first arrived that they always made sure customers who overindulged got home safely. Too much was at stake for the winery to allow someone who was visibly buzzed to get behind the wheel. Her job now was to keep them here until one of cousins came back upstairs. Ryker was standing over by the snack table. Maybe she could catch his attention, give him a little nod to bring him over as support until Bren came back upstairs.

IN ATTEMPT NOT to appear too eager, Ryker sidled over and grabbed another bottle of water from the cooler at the end of the snack table. *Festooning?* Had he actually used the word *festooning?* Sweet Lord. The woman was turning him into a complete moron. At least he'd managed to refrain from vying for her attention like the other guys had been doing. Bobby Keller had been coming on to Kitt all evening and, a couple of times, he'd seen her have to shift away from Bobby's roaming hands. He was happy to see Kitt giving equal consideration to every attendee at the workshop as she flitted from table to table.

Fortunately for Rye, Bobby realized he was getting nowhere with Kitt and had left before the event ended, heading out with Cam and Joey to catch a basketball game on the big-screen down at Hutchins House, which left only three other single guys competing for his beautiful Irish lass. He couldn't help chuckling at himself, thinking of Ms. Kathleen Boynton as *his*. They'd barely had ten minutes of conversation between them. Yet somehow, she already felt like his. His infatuation to be sure, his challenge most likely, perhaps even his Waterloo—that remained to be seen—but *his*, nonetheless.

Now, he watched as Kitt assessed the four buzzed women at the table by the fireplace. Seemed as if she was unsure about how to handle them. While the other participants of the workshop had enjoyed themselves without overindulging, he wasn't surprised to see Carol and Mari drinking too much. He'd been eyeing the table all evening, waiting to see if he was going to have to intervene. It wouldn't have been the first time he'd helped the two divorcées home after a night out, and from the dismayed look on Kitt's face, she was evidently out of her depth.

With a quick gulp of icy water, he sauntered over to the table. "Carol, Mari, how great to see you two out tonight, and you brought friends." He nodded to the other two women. "Hi, I'm Ryker Lange. You ladies look like you're having a lot of fun. I thought I heard someone say Mari was the DD tonight." He shook his head. "I don't think so, Mari."

Kitt offered him a brief smile of relief and backed away with the empties, whispering "I'll get Bren" as she left.

When Rye held out his hand for Mari's keys, she clasped her fist around them, hopped awkwardly off her stool and, swaying slightly, poked him in the chest.

Her speech slurred as she announced too loudly, "Nobody drives my car but me, bud."

Ryker took a step back, tossing a glance over his shoulder at Kitt, hurrying down the steps to the wine cellar. "I don't want to drive your car, Mari. But you're not going to drive it, either," he said, the smile never leaving his face. "Bren's going to come up here, and he and I are going to drive you ladies home."

Carol slid off her stool and stumbled before grabbing the table to keep herself upright. "C'mon, Rye. Mari's fine. She's only had a couple glasses. We're gonna go now and head down to watch the game at the double H." She yanked her purse from the back of her chair and slid her card off the table, bringing a rain of glitter and tiny candy hearts with it. "Oh, crap. Hey, anybody got a broom?"

Ryker glanced over his shoulder as Brendan Flaherty strolled up, also with a big grin on his face and said, "Ladies, it would bring me no end of pleasure to drive down Main Street with a couple of beautiful women. Who's going with me and who's going with Rye?" He plucked the keys out of Mari's hand and pocketed them so swiftly, even Ryker was startled.

Rye had to hand it to him, this was clearly not his first

buzzed-customer rodeo. "I'll take Mari and Carol, Bren, you can drive…" He looked pointedly at the two other women at the table, who had the wherewithal to appear sheepish.

"Mandy and Lisa," the older of the two offered, "and we'd appreciate a ride home. We live in Vevay."

Bren grinned even wider. "Great. If you're nice and don't hurl in my car, I'll show you a picture of my daughter, Maggie, who's ten months old and the most accomplished child on the planet." He helped them both into their winter coats and led them to the door. "Kitt, I'm taking the Jeep, okay? I'll be back in about thirty."

Ryker reached around Mari to nab her winter jacket from the back of her chair while Carol struggled into her own coat and Kitt looked on, her eyes wide.

Carol yanked her zipper up to her chin. "You can just drop us off at the double H, Rye."

The audacity of her suggestion made Kitt's eyes widen even further, but didn't surprise Rye a bit. "Nope, I'm taking you both home to sleep off your buzz. There will be other games."

Mari allowed Rye to tug her coat up over her shoulders while she gave him a poor attempt at a flirtatious pout. "You're no fun, Rye. What happened to you? You used to be fun."

With a sigh and an eye roll, Ryker took each woman by the arm. "I know, Mari, it's terrible what a boring old fart I've become." As he passed the bar, he winked at Kitt, whose expression was filled with sympathy and…was that respect? Even admiration in her blue, blue eyes?

He sure hoped so.

Chapter Five

KITT SHIVERED IN her winter jacket and pulled her knitted scarf up over her mouth and nose. Maybe walking the few blocks to work wasn't such a great idea after all, because, holy cats, it was cold. She hadn't anticipated the wind when she'd decided to walk from her apartment above Mac's garage down to the tasting room by the river. There were still five blocks to go, her fingertips were tingling, and she wasn't sure she had any feeling left in her toes.

A vehicle slowed down behind her and a short beep made her stop and turn around.

"Can I offer you a lift?" Ryker Lange leaned out the passenger-side door of...no, not his police cruiser, but rather an older, immaculately maintained black pickup truck.

Kitt hesitated. Then a big gust of winter wind nearly blew her over. It was too damn cold out here to walk to rest of the way.

She nodded and slipped into the warm cab, pulling the door closed behind her. "Thank you, Lieutenant Lange." She pulled off her gloves and held her fingers up to the heater vent on the dashboard. "I didn't realize how cold it was until

I started walking. That wee wind bites."

He put the truck in gear. "Call me Ryker. As much as I love hearing you say *left*-tenant, I'm not on duty today. Where are you headed?"

"The tasting room. I'm subbing for Sean while he and Meg go to Indy for the day."

"I'd be surprised if you got any customers today." Ryker pulled away from the sidewalk and eased the truck to the corner. "It's a little cold for wine tasting."

"I've discovered it's never too cold for wine tasting. I imagine I'll see a few good people today."

"Maybe."

Kitt glanced over at him, noticing the scruff of golden beard, the plaid flannel shirt under a puffy black winter coat, jeans, and battered cowboy boots. Apparently, it was indeed his day off. "Do you ride?"

He tossed her a quizzical look. "Ride?"

"Horses."

When his brow furrowed again, she pointed to his feet. "You're wearing cowboy boots."

He chuckled. "Oh, no, I don't ride, actually." Color rose above his collar. "I'm not some urban cowboy type, though. My brother Max gave them to me for my birthday years ago. I just like how comfortable they are."

They rode silently for another uncomfortable moment or two before he began, "Your valentine thing…"

She started, "This doesn't seem like your…"

He turned onto Riverview Road. "Sorry."

She laughed self-consciously. "No, I'm sorry. What were

you going to say?"

"I…um…I wanted to congratulate you on your event the other night. It seemed like it was a big success." His voice cracked a little. Was it possible that he was nervous, too?

"Thank you. It went well." The heady masculine scent of his soap, woods and earthy musk, filled her senses and she scooted a little closer to the door to catch her breath. "We were quite pleased."

He gave her a smile, one that set her heart thumping and made her want to both jump out of the truck and jump him. Neither was a good idea, so she kept her gaze straight ahead and edged even closer to the door.

"You started to say something." Ryker's deep voice sent a shiver through her.

She shrugged. "It was nothing."

He slowed down as they approached the tasting room car park. "No, what?"

She stared at him as he deftly made the turn into the lot in front of the cedar-and-glass building. "It was just that…this…a lorry…um, a *truck* isn't what I pictured you driving."

Ryker's expression brightened like a kid who'd found the toy he'd been longing for in his Christmas stocking. "You pictured *me?*" He pulled into a parking space in front of the tasting room, but left the engine running and turned down the fan on the heater so it wasn't blasting hot air into the already-too-warm cab.

"Don't go gettin' a big head, copper. I simply imagined you'd be driving some fancy sports car. You seem the type."

He unbuckled his seat belt, twisted on the bench seat, and extended his arm across the back. One more simple movement and his fingers would be tangled in the braid that hung below her knitted cap.

He peered at her in the close quarters of the cab, his deep voice resonating when he asked, "What type is that?"

She shrugged, scooting farther away from him to the point that she was practically sitting on the door's armrest. "You know, a fast-cars, fast-women kind of guy."

He raised one brow. "And that's who you think I am?"

"That's who I've been told you are."

"You can't believe everything you hear, sweetheart." He dropped his hand and then he *was* toying with a tendril of hair that had escaped her braid.

"Really? In your case, I think I can." The heat in the cab wasn't coming from the heater anymore. She tipped her head away from his fingers, longing to yank her scarf from around her neck and unzip her jacket. She didn't because that would have been stupid and careless and surely misinterpreted.

He sighed deeply. "What can I do to prove to you I'm not some lecherous sleaze out to rob you of your virtue? Because, truth is, I really want to have dinner with you, maybe a stroll along the River Walk."

"In this weather?" With an effort, she kept her tone light.

"Well, okay, not a stroll in this weather, but we could go to a movie or something." He widened his eyes and his perfect teeth caught his lower lip in a gesture so sensual, it made her suck in a breath.

Damn the man for being too attractive for his own good.

For *her* own good. "Tell me you didn't just bite your lip, Ryker Lange. That's so typical."

His expression was all innocence. "Did I?"

She pointed one finger at him. "You did and you know you did."

He grasped her finger and then laced his own fingers with hers. "So what if I did?" He grinned. "I'm trying to convince you to go out with me. I'm going to use whatever's in my arsenal—typical, shady, and otherwise."

She let her fingers stay linked with his for a moment, enjoying the feel of a warm male hand in hers. She'd missed that touch. But there was no way she was going to get involved with Ryker Lange. Not when his whole demeanor reminded her so much of the heartache she'd left behind in Ireland. She pulled away and folded her hands in her lap. "Have you ever been *friends* with a woman?"

He gave her an incredulous look. "What? Of course I have. I have lots of women friends."

She shook her head. "No, I'm talking about being *just* friends. Not flirting, not trying to get a date, not trying to get into her knickers." When he started to respond, she held up a hand to stop him. "And I'm not talking about women old enough to be your mother, and not your sister or your cousins either. I mean women like…well, like me."

He gave her a dazzling smile, and for maybe the twentieth time since she landed in the United States, she thought *Americans sure have perfect teeth.* "You mean women I'm attracted to?"

She snorted inelegantly. "How could ye possibly know

you're attracted to me? We've barely exchanged an hour's worth of conversation."

He leaned closer. "Don't you believe in love at first sight?"

She turned to face him. "No. As a matter of fact, I don't. I don't much believe in love at all, frankly."

His warm cinnamon-scented breath mingling with hers made her a little dizzy, but she was damned if she was going to show a moment of emotion when he murmured, "What happened to you, Kathleen?"

"I was stupid once—well, more than once—but after the last disaster...let's just say, now I'm smarter," she replied, not backing away. No way was she going let this gorgeous hunk of male intimidate her into trusting him. Not again. Not ever again. Ryker Lange was nothing more than another snake trying to slither his way into her bed. An alley cat looking for an innocent mouse to toy with. Well, she wasn't an innocent anymore. Ethan Craine had taken care of that.

She closed her eyes and when she opened them, he'd moved away and was leaning against the window, watching her. The look on his face had softened and she no longer felt like prey. However, the guy needed taken down a peg or two.

She pointed one finger at him. "I've got a challenge for ye, Lieutenant."

Ryker raised one brow. "A challenge?"

"Aye." Kitt nodded as she worked on a way to form the experiment she'd decided to put before him. "I'd like us to be friends. *Just* friends."

WHEN SHE CLOSED her eyes, Rye dropped back against his door, his bare head pressed to the icy glass. He didn't want to be in her space. He'd flirt shamelessly, but he'd never resort to caveman tactics, especially not with someone he was as attracted to as he was Kitt Boynton. "Just friends?" *This* was her challenge? Was she kidding?

"Aye." She pressed her lips together in a thin line before releasing a breath. "No flirting, no innuendo, no asking for dates, no pushing yourself on me. Just friends like…like you are with Bren or Aidan or any of the guys you work with on the police department."

He snorted a laugh. "There are women on the department, too, you know."

She flipped her hand. "Whatever. How many of them are you dating?"

"None." His conscience nudged him, so he corrected himself. "At least not recently."

Her eyes grew wider. "You've dated your fellow officers? Is that even legal?"

He chuckled. "Of course it's legal. You can't be working the same shift or the same case, but you can date other cops."

She raised one brow. "How'd that work out for you?"

He studied her curious expression for a few seconds. He could play this game. Sure. No problem. Especially if it meant he'd eventually get past her prickly defenses. "Are you asking as a friend or as a potential date?"

"As a friend, of course," she replied primly.

"It was fine. Hard to maintain a relationship when one of us worked days and the other worked nights."

"I imagine so." She snugged her scarf around her neck. "Well, thanks for the lift, Lieutenant. I appreciate it."

"When are you going to call me by my first name?" He offered what he hoped was a neutral smile, no lip-biting. "After all, don't you call your other friends by their first names?"

"I do," she conceded with a nod of her head. "Okay, thank you for the lift...Ryker."

He didn't want her to get out of the truck. The warm cab had filled with the scent of her perfume—flowers with a hint of citrus—making thinking difficult. "So, some of us are going to get together down at the double H for wings and the game tonight; want to join us? IU's playing Illinois. Both Big Ten schools that are doing well this season, so it ought to be a good matchup."

He could see the wheels turning in that gorgeous head of hers and he wished like crazy he knew what she was thinking. He gave her a few seconds to hesitate, before adding, "Not a date. Just a bunch of friends. You should meet some of the other folks in town."

He had her—he knew it and so did she. If she turned him down, the challenge was off before it began, and he was free to pursue her in any way he chose.

Finally, she sighed. "Football?"

Hope surged in him, but he tamped it down. "No, basketball."

She turned to him with a baffled look, her hands lifted,

palms up. "But I don't know anything about basketball."

"No problem. I...*we'll* teach you. If you live in Indiana, you gotta love basketball. If we had an official sport here, it would be basketball—Hoosier Hysteria is a real thing."

"Hoosier Hysteria?"

"Have you ever seen the movie *Hoosiers*?"

"No."

Rye was floored, and with all the years of being a cop under his belt, not much floored him anymore. "Your cousins have been lax in your cultural education, Ms. Boynton. You've got to see *Hoosiers*."

She gave a frustrated little moue, her full lips pursed, her blue eyes flashing. "Sorry, I've never even heard of it."

He shook his head. "Well, you can't live in Indiana and not know that film. We'll have to fix that and soon, *my friend*." He tapped the steering wheel with a knuckle. "But tonight, you watch your first game at the tavern. Tip-off is at seven."

"Tip-off?"

"The beginning of the game where the ref tosses the ball in the air and a player from each team tries to tap it away, then..." His explanation lost steam at her confused expression. "Oh, hell, it's easier to explain while it's happening. How about I pick you up here when you close at six? We can grab some food before the game starts."

She eyed him. "How many other of your friends are you picking up and buying dinner for before the game?"

"Fair enough." He tried to sound casual in spite of the knot tightening in his stomach. Apparently, she was going to be hard core about this whole not-dating thing. "Meet you there at seven. We'll be in the back room where the pool tables and the big-screen are. Grab yourself a drink at the bar on your way in. Oh, and the Tuesday night special is always wings. Butch's are the best, so order a large basket. We just stick 'em in the middle of the table and everyone enjoys."

"Fine." When she opened the door, she had to grip the handle to keep it from blowing away from her in the brisk winter breeze.

Rye struggled with his conscience, but resisted the urge to help her. He wouldn't have helped Bren or Max or any other guy. He did, however, lean over and call out to her, "Hey, Irish, leave your Amex at home. Hutchins only takes Visa, Mastercard, or cash." His words were snatched away on the wind, but he was certain she heard him because she slammed the truck door closed before spinning on her heel and stalking up the sidewalk.

Rye merely chuckled as he put the truck in gear.

Game on, Miss Boynton.

Chapter Six

THE BAR WAS crowded when Kitt walked in about fifteen minutes before "tip-off," something she couldn't even picture. Hutchins House was apparently a popular venue—there wasn't a single empty table in the main room and only a couple of open stools at the bar. A swell of homesickness rose in her chest at the sight of the dark, carved wooden bar with the huge mirror behind it. Callaghan's pub in Bally-water had the same kind of bar, except no doubt way older than the one here. She smiled thinking about Sean telling her Hutchins House, built in the mid-nineteenth century was the oldest still-operating tavern on the river. Impressive, sure, but Dublin's oldest continuously running tavern opened in 1198. History here in the States was more like current events.

"Hey, Kitt!" A deep voice drew her attention from the bar and she glanced around to see two of the men who'd attended the Pink Wine and Valentines event. Their names escaped her, but they gestured to an empty seat at their table, waving an invitation. She simply waved back, smiled, and shook her head, heading for the bar as she spotted the archway to the back room where Ryker had told her to meet him.

"Hi, gorgeous, what can I get you?" The bartender set a cardboard coaster in front her.

Kitt gave the man a slight frown. "Do you greet all your female patrons that way?"

He grinned. "I greet *everybody* that way." He tilted his head toward a large, bearded man in a plaid flannel shirt and puffy vest who sat a few stools away from where Kitt stood. "Don't I, good-lookin'?"

The lumberjack's smile showed white against his tidy dark whiskers. "You sure do, you pretty thing." He winked at the bartender and then extended his hand to Kitt. "Care to join me?"

Kitt offered a contrite smile. Somehow, her encounter with Ryker today had made her bristly. "Um, I'm meeting some people"—she gestured toward the back room, where the knocking of pool balls resonated—"back there for the game. I'd like a pint, please."

"Of what?" The bartender pulled a glass down from a rack above his head.

"Get the lady a Guinness, Hugh, don't you hear that accent?"

At the barman's quirked eyebrow, Kitt smiled. "Actually, do you have any Murphy's Irish Red?"

"No, but I have Killian's Irish Red on tap. Made in the USA from an old Irish recipe; closest I can come to a pub in Dublin."

"Sounds fine to me." Kitt perched on the edge of a bar

stool while the bartender drew the lager from the beer tap in front of him. "May I order a large basket of chicken wings, too, please?"

"Certainly." He set a shiny one-page menu in front of her. "What kind? Feel free to mix and match. Someone will bring those back to you."

Kitt perused the list of twelve—*twelve!*—different kinds of sauces and chose two that sounded pretty good.

When the barkeeper set the pint in front of her, he waved away her twenty. "First beer at Hutchins is always on the house. If you want another, we'll add it to your food tab."

The burly man frowned. "Wait a minute! I don't think *my* first beer here was on the house."

"It was, Doc, you just don't remember." The bartender chuckled. "All those years in med school and late nights at the hospital have fried your memory. Sad in one so young."

Kitt gazed at the guy next to her. "You're a doctor?"

"I am." He extended his hand. "Dr. Maxim Lange. Emergency medicine. St. Mark's, just down the street." He held up one huge hand at her smile of recognition. "I know, I know, but my mom was reading *Rebecca* while she was pregnant with me, so"—he offered a rueful shrug—"but my friends call me Max."

"I'm Kitt Boynton. I'm here visiting my cousins, the Flahertys." Kitt allowed him to engulf—there was no other word for it—her own slender fingers. The handshake was friendly and his expression curious, but kind, not wolfish, yet there was something about his gray eyes.

Lange.

The very familiar name tweaked a fuzzy memory of a brief conversation with one of her cousins. This handsome giant had to be Ryker's brother, although the two men couldn't have been more different. "You're Ryker's brother, aren't you? You look nothing like him, except your eyes." The words were out before she could stop them.

He nodded and offered a shy smile. "Guilty. But don't hold that against me, darlin'. How do you know Rye?" His dark brows drew together for a moment before the disarming smile reappeared. "Oh wait, that's right. He brought Mom to that valentine thing at the winery a few nights ago. She sure loved that."

His words warmed Kitt's heart. Feedback about the Pink Wine and Valentines event had been great, and she was delighted. Her first venture into marketing for Four Irish Brothers Winery was a success, and she took heart that the rest of her plans—an old-fashioned Valentine's Day dance, the Winemaker's Table, a spring celebration to coincide with the town's Redbud Festival, endless summer fun, and myriad other ideas—would be as well received. She only hoped her visa came through soon, so she could see all her events come to fruition. She couldn't bear the thought of going back to Ireland with her tail tucked between her legs.

"I'm terribly glad she enjoyed herself." Kitt took a sip of the ice-cold beer. *Heaven.* "Are ye watching the game?"

"Nope. I'm going to finish this beer and then head home to get some sleep, I just got off a twelve that turned into a sixteen because of a car accident up on the highway. I swear people in this state put their brains on hold at the first sign of snow." He gave her another smile, but she could see the exhaustion in his eyes. "You enjoy the game."

Kitt couldn't help returning his infectious grin. "I know nothing at all about basketball, but I promised your brother I'd come to learn."

"Rye loves basketball"—his pause was full of innuendo—"and beautiful women."

Kitt just shook her head. "So I've heard. But no bother. I'm pretty much immune to any male's charms at this point in my life."

Max chuckled. "Oh, man, you're going to be a challenge. Rye loves a challenge."

"I'm going to be his *friend*." Kitt put on her primmest expression at Max's knowing look.

"Yeah, good luck with that." He downed the rest of the beer, wiped his beard with a paper napkin, and slid off his stool. "They all fall eventually. He's the heartbreak kid."

The nickname didn't surprise Kitt in the least. "I can handle myself." Those weren't idle words. She *could* handle herself. If Ethan Craine had taught her nothing else, he'd surely taught her to protect her own heart.

SOMEHOW RYKER SENSED Kitt's presence in the tavern's noisy back room before he even saw her. His back to the doorway, he'd just glanced at his watch, wondering if she would actually show up when the nape of his neck tingled.

That had never happened to him before in his life; he swiped his palm under the collar of his red fleece jacket, thinking perhaps some bug had found its way into his shirt. Then it happened again, and he twisted around in his chair. That was when he saw her—silhouetted against the lights in the bar, a pint glass in her hand.

His heart leaped in his chest and he shoved his chair back from the table, rose to meet her, then stopped, dropped back into his chair, and merely gave her a brief wave. "Hey, Kitt."

There was no way he was going to pull out her chair, as he might have done for any other woman joining him at the battered wooden table. Nor would he bother to introduce her around, because seriously, would he have done that with a guy who walked in to watch the game?

She wants buddies, that's what she gets.

So it fell to Aidan Flaherty, Kitt's cousin, to introduce her. He pointed to the last open chair at their table with a "Guys, say hi to my cousin, Kitt. This is her first basketball game."

A chorus of greetings followed Kitt to the chair next to Rye's, which he had deliberately held open for her by casually resting his feet in the seat until she arrived. With an effort, he kept his eyes on the big-screen TV where the game was minutes from starting.

Kitt set her beer down on the table. "What's happening?"

Rye tossed her a quick glance. "Tip-off in about two minutes. The game starts when the ref throws the ball into the air in the center and a player from each team jumps up and tries to tap it away, toward their basket."

"Then what happens?"

"It's going to hit the floor or the backboard or somewhere, and one of the other players is going nab it to start the game." He allowed himself a peek at her face, which was flushed with the cold outside and adorable. Her shiny dark hair was pulled up into a high ponytail and her blue knit scarf turned her eyes even more intensely sapphire. He went on to explain the intricacies of the action on the court, all the while fighting a desire to tuck behind her perfect ear the strand of hair that had escaped the ponytail and curled against her cheek.

Aidan leaned in after IU took control of the ball, his blue eyes, exactly like Kitt's, sparking with curiosity. They really ought to name that color *Flaherty blue*, Rye thought, because every last one of them had those damn cornflower-colored eyes. "So Kitt told me she's here on a bet?"

Kitt raised one hand. "I said I challenged him, it's not a bet."

Aidan grinned. "It should be."

Ryker gulped. If word of her challenge got out, this town would run with it. "What did you tell him?"

She crossed her arms over her rounded breasts—purely a defensive move. "Only that I told you I didn't think you could just be my friend, without flirting."

Rye snorted. "I'm already doing it, babe. Did I pick you up? Buy your beer? Pull out your chair?"

Kitt gave him a sidelong look. "No, *babe*, you didn't do any of *those* things." Then she half smiled at her cousin. "See? When's the last time he called you *babe*?"

Rye's stomach fell. This was going to be harder than he first thought. "Oh, for Pete's sake, seriously?"

She smiled at him, fluttering her long, dark lashes.

He promptly pointed an accusing finger at her. "Ah-ha…eyelash fluttering—definitely flirty!"

Another way-too-innocent smile later, she replied, "I'm not the one who's not allowed to flirt."

"How's that fair?" Rye's stomach fell a few more inches. Pretty soon it was going to be down around his socks. "You can flirt with me, but I can't flirt with you? Is that how this is going to work?"

Aidan smacked a hand on the table. "I gotta go with Rye on this one, coz, that's not fair. How about this? Neither of you can flirt. Just buds."

"Yeah, and that means no calling her *babe* or *sweetheart*." This from Jean, the server who placed a huge basket of wings in front of Kitt along with six plates and a stack of napkins. "And no winking or any of those other things you do that make us all swoon." She clearly deliberately swung her very nice butt as she walked away from the table, calling to Kitt over her shoulder, "I started a tab for you, honey."

"Thank you." Kitt grinned, licked her lips at the basket of wings, and reached for a plate, oblivious to Rye's scowl.

Aidan held up a hand. "Well, Kitt can't be fluttering her eyelashes or giving him suggestive smiles."

Kitt narrowed her eyes as Rye and Aidan exchanged a high-five across the table. "Suggestive smile? When have I ever…"

Rye snickered. "Um, how about two minutes ago?"

"I don't think she should be allowed to do that strut that women do either," Noah Barker put in. He was sitting a table away with Dot and Mary Higgins and Clyde and Gloria Schwimmer.

Gloria sat back in her chair. "Well, then he can't do that pretend-buddies arm-around-the-shoulder thing that you men pull on us."

"Or the boob graze when you're reaching for the salt," added Dot with a pointed look at Noah.

Noah's eyes widened behind his thick lenses. "Whoa! I've never done that!"

"Oh, every man does that!" Mary scoffed.

"Well, she can't be using that soft voice that makes us have to lean in and—" Clyde began.

"Which gives you guys ample opportunity to look down our blouses," Teresa Ashton called from two tables away. Her husband, Frank, retired fire chief, and their grandson Nate were chowing down on wings, but clearly enjoying the exchange that pretty much seemed to include the entire room at that point as more voices chimed in with suggestions.

"No compliments from either side."

"No come-hither gazes."

"No little touches on the arm or taking her elbow."

"No late-night texts or phone calls." This from Carly Hayes, sitting quietly in the corner with Mac, who, with a side-eye to Carly, added, "And no checking in with a *what's up?* text in the middle of the day."

Rye couldn't help it, he cracked up. "I think we get it,

guys. This is *our* bet—hers and mine. We'll figure it out."

Her lips twisted slightly. "Are we seriously going to make a bet here?"

He gazed at her for a minute, realizing that just seeing her face made him want to reach for her, pull her against him, smell her hair, and press his lips to hers. What the ever-lovin' hell was going on with him? He'd asked her earlier that day if she believed in love at first sight, but it was a joke. A pickup line he'd used before. However, maybe it wasn't a line. It felt real.

Seeing the anticipation in her eyes made his heart pound like he'd just finished fighting the late spring rapids downriver in his kayak. Suddenly, he longed for a quiet bench on the River Walk where he could get to know this woman, who she was, how she became that person, her history, her dreams. Because Kitt Boynton was *The One*—that knowledge welled up in him from a deep, unfamiliar part of his being and with it, a cold clutch of panic. Unnerved, he hesitated, not sure at all of his footing. What he might or might not have wanted was of no consequence, though, because right this minute, what he had was *this*—a roomful of nosy friends and a woman with a clear challenge in her eyes.

Struggling to maintain his usual cool demeanor, he leaned back with his hands behind his head and gave her a smug smile. "Yup. I'm in if you are. If I can spend time with you and not flirt at all for"—he paused, a brilliant idea taking hold—"the next three and half weeks until Valentine's Day, then you have to agree to be my date for the dance at the winery on Valentine's night."

Kitt stopped dead in the middle of bringing a sticky chicken wing to her lips. She set the wing back on her plate and wiped her fingers on a paper napkin, her brow furrowing.

Aidan reached for the basket, dropping a couple of wings on a plate in front of him. "And Kitt, if you agree to the bet, you can't mess with him. It all has to be on the up-and-up. Two people just getting to know each other as friends with no flirting."

"And you can't spend the next three and half weeks avoiding each other either," Noah added. "If it's going to be a real bet, you gotta see each other, be together."

Rye scanned the faces of his friends, all of whom seemed way too invested in this exchange. But that was how things happened in River's Edge. It was winter, not much was going on, and this crowd would do anything for entertainment. He turned his gaze on Kitt, who still hadn't said anything. "Well?"

She pressed her lips—her full, pouty lips—in a tight line, steepled her fingers, and tapped them against her chin. "Okay. It's a bet. But here's what I want from you, if *I* win."

Rye's confidence grew. He could totally do this and whatever she wanted would be worth the chance to get to know her better. "Name it."

"If I win," she stretched out the sentence, increasing the drama, "you have to make amends to a woman you left heartbroken."

Rye's stomach fell the rest of the way—it was now officially in his socks. "*What?*"

Kitt nodded. "Not particularly the last woman you *dated*, Lieutenant, but the last woman who departed heartbroken."

He could not believe it. How the hell was he supposed to do that? "I'm not sure I know what you mean—I don't break hearts. I love women."

She quirked one brow. "Really? You don't know? 'Cause your brother just told me that around here they call you the heartbreak kid."

Rye waved that notion away with a flip of his hand. "*Pfft.* He was kidding."

Someone behind him cleared his throat...audibly...and Rye suddenly remembered that this conversation was happening in a roomful of his friends and fellow townsfolk. People who had known him his whole life. He gazed at the faces surrounding him, expectant, amused, curious, doubtful faces, each one watching him, waiting for his reaction to the metaphorical glove Kitt had just tossed down before him.

Oh, hell. He could probably figure out someone he could apologize to if it came to that. A dim memory flickered through his consciousness—a tear-marked face... He shook his head. It didn't matter. He wouldn't have to pay up because he intended to be Kitt Boynton's best buddy for the next month, and after this stupid wager was over, he'd win her heart.

He stuck out his hand. "It's a bet."

Chapter Seven

"I'D WEAR TWO pairs of socks if I were you." Sam Flaherty, Conor's wife, had settled onto the sofa in Kitt's apartment with her seven-year-old stepdaughter, Ali, curled up beside her, a fuzzy fleece blanket tucked around them as they watched Kitt finish getting dressed.

"Seriously? *Two* pairs?" Kitt was already sweltering in silk long underwear, jeans, a turtleneck, and a FOUR IRISH BROTHERS WINERY sweatshirt that Sam had brought over for her. "I put on these damn tight knickers and undershirt, I've got a flannel shirt on over those and then this heavy jumper, er, sweatshirt, plus, I've got my jacket."

Sam shrugged. "It's ice fishing, Kitt. It gets cold out there in those shacks."

"There's a shack?"

"Yes, set up on the ice."

Ali gazed at her with the kind of seriousness only a seven-year-old can give. "That means the shack floor is the ice, Aunt Kitt."

Sam dropped a kiss on Ali's dark hair. "Well, actually, there's a wooden floor and the shack is on runners, like a sled, but there is a giant hole in the center of the floor, so it's going to be cold, I promise."

"I canna believe I agreed to do this." Kitt had met Rye, his older brother, Becker, who was also gorgeous, and their mother, Jane, on the steps outside St. Agnes after church service and made the mistake of smiling and greeting them.

Ryker immediately let her know that he and a group of buddies were going ice fishing that afternoon on Green River Lake north of town. "Why don't you come, too? It's fun. Fishing's good right now, and Cam and Joey Walker's old man put a woodstove in the shack a few years ago, so it's usually halfway warm. We caught a bunch of pike and crappie last time." He gave her what could only be described as a sly look. "Just a few *buddies*, fishing on a Sunday afternoon."

Damn the man for asking her right there on the steps of the church where at least ten of the people who'd been in the bar Friday night milled about waiting to greet the pastor. It was a test. He knew it and she knew it. If she turned him down, it'd be all over town in a heartbeat that she was already backing down from the bet.

So she'd given him her sunniest smile. "Sure. Okay. Tell me how to get there and what time. I'm going to have to borrow a pole, though. I don't have one."

Rye had waved away her concern. "There's a mess of poles at the Walkers' shack and Cam usually has shad thawed for bait. You want to hitch a ride up to the lake? It's kind of off the beaten path."

"Oh, no worry, I've got GPS. I'll find it."

He'd nodded. "Okay. Cell service out there sucks, though, so if you get lost, you probably won't be able to call us."

She'd stared at him for a moment, too aware of the listening ears surrounding them. "All right. What time are you picking me up?"

He grinned triumphantly. "In about an hour and a half. Dress warm." And he'd sauntered down the steps high-fiving Noah and Clyde as he passed them on the sidewalk.

Jerk.

"Who do you think the other buddies are?" Kitt struggled into the second pair of socks, before yanking on her fur-lined winter boots.

Sam thought for a moment. "I'd say definitely Cam and Joey because they own the shack with their dad. He might be there, too. Probably Cam and Joey's cousins Jackson and Eli—they're the ones who play poker every other Wednesday night with Rye and Bren in the Walkers' party barn."

Kitt looked up from lacing her boots. "Party barn?"

Ali peeked out from her cozy cocoon in Sam's arms. "It's an awesome place, Aunt Kitt! Emily Walker and I had our birthdays together there the last two summers. Birthdays six and seven, 'cause I'm seven now and this summer coming up, I'll be eight."

Kitt couldn't help smiling at the little imp; she reminded her so much of her sister Nora when she was that age.

"It's a venue that Jack and Eli built from Eli's parents' old barn—they both work at Walker Construction, too. They do a lot of weddings and parties and stuff like that there all summer," Sam explained. "They have hog roasts and barbecues; all kinds of fun events. We've worked with them and so has the wine trail a few times. You should meet those two, especially if you end up staying to do events for the winery."

Boots tied, Kitt rose and pulled on her knit cap, tucking her hair behind her ears, and then coated her lips with protective balm. "Do I need my purse?"

"Nah, just stick your lipstick, wallet, and phone in your jacket pocket. Oh, and grab that bottle of sani over there"— Sam pointed to a purse-sized bottle of hand sanitizer on the counter—"and some tissues. I don't think there's a proper bathroom out there, only a porta-potty."

Kitt frowned. "Great. Sounds lovely."

Sam simply smiled. "You're doing this for women everywhere, Kitt. Be brave." She tossed off the throw and bundled Ali into her winter coat before slipping into her own. "Come on, kiddo, I imagine Daddy is ready for us to come home. He's been alone with Griff and Liam since church got out, plus he wanted to go up the winery with Uncle Sean and check the tanks."

"I thought Sunday was supposed to be Daddy's day off in the wintertime," Ali grumbled as she zipped her coat.

A horn blared outside and Kitt peered out the window to see a big black truck in the driveway below. "This is it. That's Ryker. Cleansing breath." She inhaled deeply, then released the air slowly.

Sam's eyes widened. "He's *honking* at you?"

"I'm one of the guys, remember?" Kitt wrapped her scarf

around her throat and tucked the ends into her jacket.

"Why do you look so scared, Aunt Kitt?" Ali tugged on her mittens. "Fishing is fun and Loo-Lootelant Lange is a policeman. Policemen are our friends."

Kitt shook her head as she herded Ali and Sam out the door and locked it. "You are absolutely right, lambie. I hope I catch a big fish." She narrowed her eyes at Sam, who grinned up at her as they made their way down the steps to the driveway where Ryker waited. "Don't say it."

Sam chuckled and pretended to draw a zipper across her lips. "I didn't say a word."

"You didn't have to. I saw it on your face." She pulled open the passenger door, managed the high step up, and slid into the seat next to Ryker without incident.

"Hi, Rye! Have fun, you guys." Sam waved as she supervised Ali getting into the booster seat in the back of her car, parked in front of Ryker's truck in the driveway.

Kitt pulled the seat belt across her body and snapped it into place. "How long do kids have to use booster cushions here?"

Ryker lowered his sunglasses—simple plain gray lenses in a black frame, not the mirrored aviators Kitt had suspected—and stared at her for a few seconds. "Good morning to you, too, Kitt."

"It's afternoon."

"Whatever." He sighed, put the truck in gear, backed down the driveway, and headed toward Sixth Street, which Kitt realized was not the way north out of town. "Kids younger than eight must be in some kind of child safety seat," he said. "However, we recommend they stay in the back and restrained in a proper system until they're at least forty pounds and forty-eight inches tall."

Kitt turned in her seat when they passed the road that she was certain would take them north. "Where are we going? I thought the lake was north of town—I looked on a map. We're heading east."

He pulled into the parking lot of a grocery store Kitt had never been to before. "We're going to grab some snacks." He parked and turned off the truck. "Don't worry. I'm not abducting you."

She pressed her lips tightly together to keep from grinning. "I wasn't worried. Friends don't abduct friends." She reached for the door handle, then turned her most innocent smile on him. "Right?"

He nodded shortly.

Kitt followed him into the store as he made no effort whatsoever to defer to the usual cordialities a man afforded a woman. Trailing behind him, she couldn't help but notice how nicely his jeans fit and wondered if he was wearing long underwear like she was. His broad shoulders in the black puffy jacket drew her eyes upward to where his blond hair curled slightly over his plaid scarf. He had thick hair. Good hair. Touchable hair.

"You'd better pick out something to snack on—we'll probably be out there until close to supper."

She stopped by the stacks of six- and twelve-packs. "Should I bring some beers?"

He glanced up from a display of jerky. "If you want

some."

"What kind do you like?"

He eyed her for a moment, as if he was trying to decide. "Get what *you* like. I don't drink."

That was unexpected. "You don't drink beer or you don't drink at all?"

"At all." He grabbed a six-pack of lemonade, a handful of beef sticks, and a couple of bags of chips and headed for the register, where he snatched several candy bars. "Move it, we have to pick up another couple of other guys."

Kitt frowned, shrugged, and picked up a six-pack of her favorite cherry cola instead of beer and a bag of peanuts. Scurrying to the checkout, she tossed her items on the belt with his. "I've got this. You're driving." She whipped her Visa out of her wallet and swiped it before Rye could reach into his back pocket.

He gave her a dose of perfect white teeth. "Thanks, buddy."

"You bet, *pal*." She turned to the checkout girl. "Paper, please."

The cashier stuffed everything except the colas into a brown paper sack, which Rye left for Kitt to carry out to the truck. She shook her head. He really was taking this whole buddies bit to the extreme, but she was damned if she was going to cave first. Didn't matter how cute his grin was or how that swagger made her mouth water.

"Okay, maybe none of my business, but why don't you drink?" When Kitt snapped her seat belt into the clip, her hand brushed Rye's. Even through the insulated gloves, the touch sent a spark through her.

Rye hitched one shoulder as he turned the key in the ignition. "I'm not sure we're good enough friends yet to tell you that story."

Now Kitt's curiosity was piqued. "Are you...are you in recovery?"

He chuckled and eased the truck out into the street. "No, that's not it. Just a personal choice." The quirked brow he gave her shut her up, which she was certain was his intent.

They rode in silence until he pulled into River Run Mobile Home Park a little farther east of town. A community filled with what Kitt knew as *static caravans*, but *mobile home* worked, too.

"Who lives here?"

"Friends." Ryker drove through the rows of homes, some newer, some older, a few a little run-down, stopping in front of one particularly well-kept mobile. The deck was cleared of snow, as was the short driveway. He honked the horn and peered out the windscreen.

Two identical young boys, not yet teens as far as Kitt could tell, tumbled out the door. One of them shushed the other and carefully pulled the door shut. As cold as it was, the boys didn't have on hats or gloves.

Rye opened his door and stood on the running board. "Back in the house and get your gloves and hats, you two doofuses. It's cold out here."

"We're fine," they chorused, heading for the truck.

Rye simply pointed at them. "I got you both new hats and gloves last week. Go get them."

They came around the truck and stood by Ryker's open door. The one with the longer hair jutted out his bottom lip. "*He* took 'em."

RYE CURLED HIS fingers into a fist, but resisted punching the roof of his truck. "Dammit," he muttered and jerked his head toward the seat behind Kitt. "Get in. Buckle up." He slammed the door shut and peeled out, finding some small measure of satisfaction in knowing that in the spring, Jed Cochran would have to pick rocks out of his perfectly manicured yard, which he took much better care of than he did his two stepsons, Caleb and Josh Davis.

Damn that son of a bitch. It didn't matter what Rye gave the twins, their asshole stepfather took it from them. With a sigh, he pointed to the Target bag in the well next to Kitt's feet. "Toss that back there, would you, Kitt?"

Kitt did as he asked, bewilderment showing in her expression.

It took some effort, but he managed to smile at the kids in the rearview mirror. "New hats and gloves." His voice was strained. "When I bring you home this afternoon, hide them in your coat sleeves, okay?"

Kitt eyed him. "How did you know?"

"Experience."

"Awesome! Pacers!" Josh cried, pulling knit hats out of the sack. "And Colts!"

"I want the Colts." Caleb snatched the royal-blue cap

away from his brother.

Rye glanced over his shoulder. "Share, you two. And for Pete's sake, try not to act like the heathens you are in front of my new friend. Kitt, these two hooligans are Caleb and Josh Davis, my little brothers. Guys, this is Kitt Boynton. Show her some manners."

The one in the Colts hat scowled. "You brought a date fishing with us?"

"She's not a date, Caleb. Just a friend."

The boys hooted, but quieted down at Kitt's greeting.

"Hi, boys." Kitt twisted in her seat to face the two boys. "Quite glad to meet you." She was clearly dying of curiosity. "I'm glad you have on different hats or I'd never figure which of ye was which."

"You from Australia?" Josh shook his too-long stringy hair out of his eyes before pulling the Pacers cap down to his brow line.

"Ireland."

"We're Rye's good deed." Caleb tugged on his new gloves.

"Caleb, don't be a jerk." Rye turned the truck toward Green River Lake, choosing his words carefully as he explained the Big Brothers program to Kitt, who managed to look both impressed and perplexed all at one time.

Rye rarely talked about his work with kids, so he had surprised himself when he invited Kitt along fishing knowing he'd have the twins with him, but the urge to be with her trumped his need for circumspection. Unlike Caleb's assertion, the twins were not his *good deed*—they were much more. He'd taken them on after Father Mark had shared their story with him. Their father was killed in a motorcycle accident six years ago when the boys were six years old. Afterward, their mother, Lori, found comfort from her grief at the bottom of a tequila bottle and paid scant attention to her twin sons. He'd built a solid relationship with the boys, taking them to ball games, camping, hiking, fishing, and simply being a strong male presence in their lives for the last three years.

Recently, though, Lori married Jed Cochran, a man fifteen years her senior, who enabled her drinking, although Rye had no proof of that. Not yet, anyway. Granted, Jed had fixed up the dilapidated trailer Lori and the boys were living in, kept food on the table, and the utilities going. At first, Rye had been happy that Lori found someone who seemed to care about her and the twins. However, in the months since she and Jed had married, the boys had gradually become closed up again, reverting to the secret sign language the two of them shared, and canceling plans with Rye more frequently. It seemed to Rye that their stepfather ran the household rather like a Dickensian boys' school.

Last time he'd managed a Saturday with them, Caleb had reported that Jed had made Josh quit school choir after the Christmas program on Aidan and Holly Flaherty's restored riverboat, something the kid loved, because *only pussies sang in a choir*. Rye had intended to talk to Cochran, but Josh had begged him not to because then Jed would never let them go to the *River Queen* again. Rye had agreed reluctantly; however, he bit the inside of his cheek as he glanced in the rearview mirror and saw the boys signing to one another. Something was going to have to be done about Jed Cochran.

Rye tilted his chin toward Kitt. "You like country music?"

Her shoulders lifted. "Um, a bit. I'm not really very familiar with it."

Rye snapped on the new Bluetooth stereo he'd installed in the old truck when he discovered Josh's singing ability and handed his phone to Kitt. "Here, find Brooks and Dunn."

"No! Not those old guys." Josh leaned as far forward has he could, given his seat belt. "Old Dominion!"

"Luke Combs!" Caleb added.

Rye's heart smiled. He knew how to bring those two around—music. "Old guys?" He faked horror in the rearview mirror. "Brooks and Dunn are classic country, dudes."

Kitt chuckled as she cued up the music on his phone and scrolled through the list. "Oh, here's Old Dominion. I'm going to trust Josh and Caleb on this." With a saucy grin, she tapped the song and the opening guitar riff to Old Dominion's "One Man Band" came through the speakers as the twins cheered.

When Rye took his eyes off the road long enough to fake-glare at her, the boys cracked up and Kitt simply batted her eyelashes at him. He aimed one finger at her. "And there's the eyelash thing. I'm reporting you."

She thumbed her nose at him. "To whom? The flirting police?" Then she turned to Josh and Caleb, who were singing lustily along with Old Dominion's Matt Ramsey about how much he didn't want to be in a one-man band.

"Wow, you guys are great singers!"

Rye caught the boys' pleased expressions in the rearview mirror and tossed a grateful smile to Kitt. Not only for stepping right up with the twins, but also for not asking a lot of questions. There was time enough to share their story—and his—with her.

Chapter Eight

R YE GRITTED HIS teeth for at least the fiftieth time since he, Kitt, and the twins had gotten to Green River Lake. *What the ever-lovin' hell anyway?*

Right off, enough guys showed up that they were packed into the fishing shack like sardines in a can. All four of the Walker cousins—Cam, Joey, Jack, and Eli—were shoving the shack off the shore when he pulled into the parking area with his own crew. Eli didn't even like fishing, yet there he was, yucking it up with his cousins, his dark red hair gleaming in the sunlight that filtered through the trees. All the Walkers had that auburn hair—it was practically their trademark—and when he glanced at Kitt, she was smiling in obvious appreciation at four muscular men sliding a ten-by-ten fishing shack onto the ice. Bobby was there, too, and so were Cary and Chaz.

Eight large adult males, one very hot Irish lass, and two squirrely twelve-year-olds were simply way too many people in an ice-fishing hut, especially when most of them were falling all over each other to make sure Kitt Boynton was happy. Not flirting outrageously, his conscience nudged him, however, definitely vying for her attention and treating her like a woman in their midst rather than one of the guys— something he couldn't do because of the damn wager he'd entered into in a moment of real stupidity a couple of nights earlier. What had he been thinking? The first time in his life he'd been totally bowled over by a woman and he'd blown it with a stinking just-friends bet. Okay, it was only for less than a month, but dammit, he wanted her *now*. And he sure as hell didn't want Cary or Eli or any of the other single men in town getting the jump on him. His head throbbed, so he closed his eyes and leaned back against the cold wall of the shack. He opened them immediately, though, because he couldn't stand not looking at her.

And there was Cary, shoving Eli aside to get closer to Kitt while Jack firmly kept his place so close behind her a slip of paper wouldn't have fit between them. Bobby had given up early in the game and was pouting in the corner, sucking down brews. Chaz and Joey both knelt on the canvas on the side of the hole they'd sawed in the ice, so focused on Kitt, they were barely paying attention to their own lines.

Rye cleared his throat. "Um, Chaz, I think you've got a bite there."

Chaz's eyes, glazed from staring at Kitt, met his over the fishing hole. "Huh?" Suddenly he became aware of his pole bending at the tip. "Oh, crap! I've got a bite!" He no more than got the words out than the pole straightened again, the weight gone as the fish got free, something that ordinarily would've set Chaz to turning the air blue. This time, he simply shrugged with a fake self-conscious snicker, reeled in the empty line, and rebaited his hook.

An endless tumble of emotions spilled through Rye as Kitt basked in male attention. She was so open and friendly—her smile warmed the hut like they'd stoked the old woodstove to its fullest. Yet, she held back the playful part that most women would have used to their complete advantage of being the only female in a hut full of guys. She wasn't aiming for any of them, and the more the other men tried to charm her, the cooler her responses were. What had happened to her in Ireland that made her so determined not to let another man into her heart? Pondering the question, he brought his own line in, pulled off the bait, dropped the shad into the water, and set the hook into a guide eye on his pole. He hadn't caught anything, and his mind was not on fishing.

"Why are you glaring at Jack?" Josh elbowed him in the ribs.

"I'm not glaring." At least he was *trying* not to glare as Jack stood behind Kitt, his arms around her, his fingers helping her reel in what turned out to be a pretty nice-sized walleye.

"Look, look!" Kitt bounced daintily on the balls of her feet—a trick in her thick-soled, fur-lined boots—and held her fish up over the hole in the ice. "I caught one!" She turned to Jack, who was practically drooling on her hat. "What is it, Jack?"

"It's a walleye," Rye jumped in before Jack could open his mouth. "They're good eating."

"No, no. I don't want to *eat* it. That means we'll have to

kill it." Kitt dangled the silvery fish.

All the guys chuckled, and Jack tipped his face toward hers, getting way too close to those luscious lips, in Rye's opinion. "Sorry, sweetheart, that's usually the way it works. I'll take it if you don't want it."

"No!" Kitt leaned away from him. "I'm releasing it. Can someone show me how to take it off the hook?"

Seven guys jumped up and crowded around Kitt, but it was Caleb, fishing quietly on a wooden box across the hole from her, whose eyes she met. "Caleb? Can you show me how to do this without hurting him too much?"

What a kind gesture! The jealousy that had been spasming in Rye's chest all afternoon dissolved as Caleb's eyes lit up and the boy stepped around the hole to take her pole. She met Rye's gaze over Caleb's head and the expression on her face nearly doubled him over. Her heart was aching for the twins, it was written plainly in her quiet smile as she paid careful attention to Caleb's instructions, and together, they released the fish.

Rye received another sharp elbow to the ribs from Josh, who was sharing an old wooden bench with him. "Looks like you're not the only one who's crushing on Kitt," the boy said softly behind his hand.

When Rye shot him a frown, Josh just grinned. If they hadn't been packed into a fishing hut with ten other people, he'd have called the kid out; instead, he gave him the stink eye and checked his watch. Enough was enough. They'd been here for three hours, and Kitt had been slobbered over by every other male present. In addition to a headache, Rye was developing a bad case of claustrophobia, and his feet were freezing. "Caleb. Come on. We need to get you guys home. I promised your mom I'd have you home by five thirty and it's already five. We've gotta go."

Caleb's skinny shoulders drooped as Kitt reeled in her hook and unwound herself from the group of guys surrounding her. "That's my ride, guys. It's been fun!"

"Aw, Kitt…stay. I'll drive you home." This from Chaz, who'd finally managed to get to the front of the pack. He put a hand on her shoulder as she headed for the rack of poles. Rye clenched his fists.

Bobby piped up from the corner where he'd settled back onto the box with his six-pack. "Or I can."

She really shouldn't accept that offer; he's had way too many beers to be driving.

"Bobby, my man, did you forget you came with me?" Cary grabbed Bobby's knit hat and popped him on the head with it. "There's still plenty of room for one more in my truck, Kitt. We'd be glad to give you a lift if you want to stay and fish some more."

Rye got busy herding the boys into their gloves and hats, helping them put their poles up, and nabbing the leftovers from the booty he and Kitt had bought at Deke's. This was her call. He wasn't going to beg her to ride home with him, although the urge to do exactly that was forcing him to bite his tongue when she appeared to be wavering. The others had all put on their puppy-dog faces and she still hadn't racked the pole.

Caleb settled the issue by grabbing the pole from Kitt's

gloved fingers. "Come on, Kitt. We gotta roll."

With a smile that would disarm a pride of charging lions, Kitt simply shrugged and tugged her knit hat farther down on her head. "Sorry, guys. Thanks so much for letting me fish with you. 'Twas brilliant!"

KITT SAT IN the warm cab of the truck as Rye walked the boys up to the mobile, where their mother, a rather tired-looking woman who could have been any age between thirty-five and fifty, waited. He'd had the boys tuck their new hats and gloves into their sleeves before they got out, so the breeze blew their dark hair and turned the tips of their ears red. They'd both been so sweet with their goodbyes after asking her dozens of questions about her life in Ireland on the way home and then begging her to join Rye when he came to their basketball game at the junior high later that week. She'd hadn't agreed to *that* game, but assured them she'd come to see them play before the season was over.

"Who takes their belongings from them?" Rye had barely gotten his door shut when she asked the question.

"Their stepfather."

Kitt recalled the dour-faced man who'd peered out the curtained window when they had picked up the boys. "Why does she stay with him?"

"He's stable, responsible, gets the bills paid, keeps the boys in shoes and food." When he set his jaw, a muscle moved in his cheek. "And her in tequila."

Rye cared so much about the boys. It was plain in the fond way he ruffled their hair and the firm hand he'd placed on their shoulders as he walked them to the door. "Why does he take their stuff away? What does he want with their winter hats and gloves?"

He snorted. "Jed only nabs the stuff *I* give them. Those hats and gloves will show up at the station house on Monday, with a strongly worded note about how *he* can take care of his own kids. He doesn't have the balls to face me—it'll be just a bag on my desk."

"He doesn't like that you are in their lives?"

"Not one bit." He unclenched ever so slightly. "That *is* one area where Lori stands up to him, though. She insists they stay in the Big Brother program, so I get to see them once a week."

Without thinking, Kitt reached out and placed her hand on his arm. "He's jealous. Those boys are crazy about you. You can see it."

And she could. Caleb and Josh had clung to Ryker all afternoon, joking and laughing with him, listening to his fishing advice, even closing up the snack bags when he declared they'd had enough. She'd been surprised when the thought occurred what a good father he'd make. Of course, she'd dismissed the notion the moment it had popped into her head. What did it matter that Ryker Lange was great with kids? Or that he was kind? Or funny? Or compassionate? Or incredibly masculine and film-star handsome?

She caught herself ogling him…again, and when he glanced down, she realized she'd left her hand on his arm way longer than necessary.

She dropped her hand in her lap. "You're a good person, Lieutenant."

Dull color rose above the collar of his fleece vest and he shrugged. "You do what you can."

In spite of myriad questions racing through her head, Kitt kept the conversation neutral for the rest of the ride to her apartment, talking ice fishing and laughing at his story about a time he and his brothers had gone ice fishing when they were kids and didn't know what size hole to cut in the ice. His older brother, Becker, had cut three holes barely big enough to drop a line into and when Ryker caught a fish, he couldn't bring it up.

"We ended up desperately trying to cut a bigger hole. Our saw was an old rusty wood thing we'd found in the shed behind our trailer. Beck sawed and sawed while that poor fish was flailing around under the ice. I couldn't stand it. I finally just cut the line and let it swim away dragging about ten inches of nylon line. Old guy may still be out there, telling this story to his guppy grandkids." Rye flashed that snow-white smile as he pulled into Mac's driveway.

It was time to get out of his truck, but she was so warm and content there laughing with him that she hated to open the door to the bitter wind blowing outside. She had to, didn't she? Because buddies didn't linger in each other's company. They said good-bye and hopped out. Maybe a "thanks for the ride." So it was time to go.

She sneaked a side-eye peek at Ryker, who was staring straight ahead as if his whole attention was focused on the shriveled brown plant clinging to the arbor next to the Mac's garage.

She had to say *something*. "Do ye want to take the peanuts with you?"

"No, no. They're yours. And these sodas." He reached in the bag and pulled out two cans of cherry soda and the half-empty bag of peanuts and handed them to her. "Oh, and here, take a couple of the candy bars and one of these bags of pretzels."

She demurred as she grasped the bag of peanuts, trying not to let it open up and spill all over the tidy interior of his vehicle. "I'd best not. You keep them. I'd just as well *apply* them to my hips as eat them. That's where they'll end up anyway."

He laughed, a deep, happy sound that filled the truck. "Are you kidding? Why would you worry about that? You're gor—" He stopped so quickly, almost as if someone had slapped their hand over his mouth. Without ceremony, he dropped the candy and pretzels back into the brown bag on the seat between them. "Okay. I'll take them."

"What were you going to say?"

He shook his head. "Doesn't matter."

"Ryker…" There had to be something to say that wouldn't be misinterpreted as flirting or like she was trying to catch him up, but she was damned if she knew what it was. This bet was already turning out to be harder than she ever imagined.

He gave her a quick nod. "Good night, Kitt."

"I-I had fun." She opened the door a crack, holding onto

it so the wind wouldn't grab it out of her hand. "Thanks for taking me... and for introducing me to Caleb and Josh. They're great kids."

"You're welcome. See ya around."

"Yeah. See you." She slipped out, shoved the door shut, and raced up the steps to her apartment, nearly dropping one of the cans of soda in the process while Ryker backed out of the driveway so fast, his tires spun on the ice by the street.

Two cups of hot cocoa later, Kitt was curled up on the sofa, already snug in her PJs, doing the only thing she could do when she was desperately attracted to a man that she *absolutely* did not want to be attracted to. She'd called Maeve in Dublin and thank God for international calling because they'd been talking for forty-five minutes.

"Kitt, me darlin' sister, you've got to get over your thing about men. Two bad relationships are not an omen for the next one." Maeve was probably exhausted. It was six hours later there, so seven P.M. in River's Edge meant one in the morning in Dublin. But she'd answered the phone, bless her, and no doubt crept out to the lounge to keep from disturbing Declan.

"I don't trust my judgment anymore." Kitt took another sip of lukewarm cocoa. "And even though this guy is delicious and an upstanding citizen and he seems very kind, he has a reputation around town for being a player. I can't do another player. I don't have the emotional energy to deal with that."

"At least this one's single," Maeve offered around a yawn.

"Not funny, Mae."

"Look. Just get through the stupid bet. I can't believe you let yourself get drawn into that—so typical. You never could back down from a challenge." Maeve giggled. "Remember when Peter O'Malley bet you couldn't jump Paddy Gallagher's pasture fence? You did it, even though you and Dewey hadn't jumped anything higher than a fallen log before that."

"And if you'll recall, it was about to storm that day in a country that rarely ever sees thunderstorms. A clap of thunder later, I ended up on my arse in a pile of cow shite and had to chase Dewey for half a kilometer in the pouring rain because he was terrified." Kitt set her cup down, settled deeper into the sofa, and pulled the fleece throw up to her neck. "You've made my point. I have no judgment. Apparently, I never did."

"Well, ye canna stop living, Kitt. You're barely turned thirty. At some point you're going to have to take a chance again."

"As if coming to America isn't chance enough? I upended my whole life."

"To get away from some bastard rat who lied to ye." Maeve's tone softened across the miles of satellites. "And are you regretting leaving?"

Kitt considered for a moment before whispering, "No."

"I meant take a chance on love again."

"I *know* what you meant."

"I can tell how attracted you are to this copper. Let him win the bet, then loosen up and see where it goes. It's wonderful when you find the right person, Kitten. Truly."

Maeve spoke from experience, too. The love between her and Declan shone with a pure light that Kitt had basked in regularly back in Ireland.

"I'm sure it is," Kitt admitted, smoothing her fingers over the fleecy blanket. "However, I think what you and Declan have is rare in this world. And no, I'm not *letting* him win the bet. We shook on it. We have to do this fair and square. Besides, from where I'm sitting, the delectable Lieutenant Lange wouldn't know true love if it smacked him over the head, and I can't, Mae. I can't bear the thought of getting my heart broken again."

Chapter Nine

KITT PEERED THROUGH the windscreen of Bren's old Jeep, then checked her phone's GPS again. The map said she'd arrived, so this must be the place, although it wasn't at all what she'd expected. *This* was the American version of a horse farm? The place looked more like the plantation from that old movie Ma loved so much, *Gone with the Wind.* The long gravel driveway curved in front of a huge white-pillared, red-brick mansion—Kitt half expected to see a footman in a black livery rush down the steps to open her car door. The yard was perfectly manicured, even for winter, and the board fences around the distant fields impeccably maintained.

A barn three times the size of the one on the humble farm where she grew up loomed behind the house. It was painted white instead of the traditional red, and she could only imagine what it was like inside. No dirt aisle down the center, of that she was certain. Trudy Morrow's Tennessee Walkers and quarter horses probably trod on some kind of a fancy soft floor made of rubber. Surely there were no chew marks from nervous horses on the stall doors or bales of hay stacked near the tack room or manure forks resting against a wall. Kitt was sure every tool in Trudy's barn had a proper hook and you could eat off the tack room floor.

Trying not to feel intimidated, she marched up the steps and rang the bell, which echoed through a vast foyer she could see through the sidelights by the door. The man who answered seemed rather irritated she'd interrupted his morning newspaper and coffee—he'd carried both to the door with him.

"Yes?" The word was clipped.

"I'm Kitt Boynton. Trudy's expecting me." When he merely stared at her from under bushy gray eyebrows, she expanded, "I'm supposed to ride with her today."

He blinked. "Gertrude's up at the barn with the police. Someone broke into the tack room last night." He waved the paper and pointed to the driveway, nearly spilling his coffee in the process. "You can drive around there if you want." He stepped back and shut the door in her face.

Well, okay, that's that.

The barn doors were open and Kitt heard a dog bark, then voices as she got out of the Jeep, so she followed them, noting the police car parked nearby. When she walked into the barn, she had to smile—it was as immaculate as she'd expected. The aisle way was beyond neat, with lovely wooden tack boxes beside each stall and shiny brass hangers for bridles and halters above them. And sure enough, the floor was some kind of black composite material and not a single wisp of hay or sawdust to be seen. Her smile grew as she imagined what Da would say about the spotless conditions in

Trudy's barn.

Aye and I'm sure the horses are worryin' about whether there's piss on the floor or hay dust in the corners.

God, how she missed him. Missed the horses. Missed Ireland. Leaving had been the right thing, because Ethan wouldn't stop calling her, insisting he loved her and was asking his wife for a divorce.

Sure you were, you wanker.

Her Dublin friend Carrie had emailed her just the other night that she'd seen him and his perfect little family at the theater, and he'd gone white when she'd slowed down as she passed their seats. Kitt had blocked him on her phone and email, so if he was still trying to contact her, she didn't know about it. Better that way. Loneliness had her in its grip and she was still too vulnerable to risk talking to him. Wasn't the whole point behind accepting Trudy Morrow's invitation today to make new friends and salve the pain still haunting her?

She inhaled deeply and bent down to pat the little white terrier who'd raced down the aisle to greet her. Stroking the dog's soft ears, she scanned the cavernous space around her. No matter how perfect a barn was kept, you couldn't disguise the scent of horseflesh, manure, and hay. Kitt was home. She walked in farther and touched the wheelbarrow a quarter full of manure and the fork that sat outside one of the stalls. Trudy must have been cleaning stalls when she discovered the break-in.

As she drew closer to the open tack room door, she recognized the deep voice speaking over a higher, frustrated one. "Just make a list of everything that's missing, Trudy."

"Dammit, Rye, they took my show saddles, all four of the ones I won for barrel racing. And they took the dressage saddle and the jumping saddle I bought last summer. I'd started Penny over low hurdles in the fall—she was doing so great and…" Trudy's voice choked before she cleared her throat. Kitt could almost picture her straightening her small shoulders. "Well, at least they didn't hurt the horses or set the barn on fire. Remember the fire at that barn down near Lexington? They cleaned out the tack, stole the trailer, released the horses, and set the place on fire."

Kitt sidled closer and watched as Rye walked toward the door.

Damn, he's a looker.

"I remember." He was writing in a notebook as he spoke. He bent down to study the door frame. "Looks like they used a crowbar, gave it up, and kicked the door in. Quite a trick given the steps. I'm surprised they didn't fall on"—he caught Kitt's eye where she stood at the bottom of the two steps up to the tack room—"oh, hello there."

Heat filled her cheeks. "Hi." She gave him a little wave as Trudy appeared behind him.

"Oh, Kitt!" She swiped tears from her cheeks. "I'm so sorry. I should have called you. Someone broke in here last night and took all the saddles and a lot of the bridles and a bunch of other tack. I'm heartsick."

Rye rose and allowed Kitt to pass into the spacious tack area, which was every bit as spotless as the rest of the barn. Thankfully, the thieves didn't trash the place, merely removed any items of real value. Even though she didn't know her very well, Kitt acted on instinct, embracing the older woman for a brief moment. She met Rye's approving expression over Trudy's shoulder before releasing her. "No worries. I'm so sorry, Trudy. What can I do to help you?"

Rye closed his notebook. "Trudy, did you hear anyone pull in last night?"

Trudy massaged her temples. "No, we didn't, and that's weird because Todd is a light sleeper. He hears everything, even a raccoon shuffling on the gravel, and Buster here"— she swept her hand at the little dog who was sniffing Kitt's legs—"never made a sound. He always barks if someone comes up the drive, especially if they come around here to the barn. He's very protective of the horses. That's why he barked when Kitt drove up."

Rye patted Trudy on the shoulder. "I'm going to go out and look around in the barn. See if I can figure out how they got in and out without disturbing anyone, including Buster here." He knelt down to chuff the dog under the chin and stroke his head, sending Buster into paroxysms of joy. The little dog pushed his head against his wide palm and placed his paws on his knee. Rye petted him for a bit longer before he rose, closed up his notebook, and shoved it into an inside pocket of his parka.

Kitt couldn't help noticing he wasn't wearing a uniform; rather, he was dressed up in navy pants, a button-down oxford, and a striped tie. His badge was clipped to his belt and a tan corduroy blazer showed beneath his heavy winter coat. When he stood up, he had imprints of Buster's paws on the knee of his trousers. Resisting the urge to bend down and brush them away, she instead turned to Trudy. "Let me help you with your barn work. I haven't mucked a stall since I left Ireland."

"You don't have to do that. We can still ride." She motioned for them to follow her out of the tack area. "I have a couple of old trail saddles in my trailer in the garage. I'll go get them." She grabbed an empty wheelbarrow leaning against the wall and headed out.

"I'm going to clean stalls for her." Kitt picked up the wheelbarrow that already had a small pile of manure in it and pushed it to the next occupied stall.

Rye trailed a few feet behind her, passed, and made his way down the aisle, moving his head back and forth as he examined the floor. When he reached the other end, he got out his pen and touched the latch on the heavy sliding door.

What is he looking for?

He waved at her. "Hey, Kitt. C'mere."

She trotted down to where he stood. "What?"

He pointed to the latch. "Should this be open?"

She peered at it and shrugged. "Maybe. If she's dumped manure outside this door this morning. But"—she glanced around, remembering the wheelbarrow had been placed right next to the first occupied stall and the small amount of manure in it—"I don't think she's dumped anything yet."

Something wasn't right. It was too cold for Trudy to have opened the other end of the barn yet and there were no horses in the last few stalls, so no reason for her to have been down there feeding or cleaning stalls. She stepped away and scanned the floor. "Are those muddy footprints?"

Rye backed up, then knelt down to inspect where she was pointing. "Looks like it." He shook his head. "Not in Trudy Morrow's barn. And look, tire tracks."

"Want me to open the door?" She reached out, hovering her gloved hand over the latch.

"Let me shove it open from over here, but I suspect we're going to find a lot of footprints and tire tracks." When he opened the door, sunlight streamed in and sure enough, the ground right behind the barn was a muddy mess of tire tracks and footprints. Big booted footprints. The rest of the mud lot was merely hoofprints.

Kitt gazed out across the mud lot. "The gate is open on the mud lot. They must have driven in from the back field."

"And they were driving a damn big dually. Look, double tire tracks." Rye rocked back on his heels on the edge of the barn floor, clearly reluctant to step out into the lot.

Kitt didn't blame him. He had on really nice brown loafers. She had on her riding boots, so she stepped out, neatly avoiding the tire tracks in the mud. Trudy's manure pile was actually a composting area over to the side surrounded by a tall wooden fence with two big gates.

"What did you find?" Trudy hollered from the front of the barn as she shoved a wheelbarrow full of saddles before her.

"Looks like they drove in from your field." Rye pointed out the wide-open doorway. "We can drive back and take a look if your truck can make it through."

Kitt had to smile. The poor guy really didn't want to

walk through the mud lot or the field.

Trudy tapped one hand on the top saddle. "My truck's at Brown's getting the transmission worked on. I'll saddle up Ladd and Jasper and Penny and we'll ride back. You can borrow a pair of Todd's old riding boots from the tack room. You guys are probably pretty close to the same size."

RYE'S HEART DAMN near stopped. *Ride back there?* Was she kidding? Nope, she was serious. She'd unloaded two flat leather saddles from the wheelbarrow and was about to grab a bigger cowboy-style one along with a couple of dark maroon quilted pads.

"Um, Trudy, I'm not really dressed to ride." He held open his parka so she could see he was wearing nice pants and a blazer.

"Ah, you'll be fine. We'll tuck your pants down into the boots." She spoke over her shoulder and as she headed up the steps into the tack room, but her voice carried out into the barn. "Here we go—and there's even a clean pair of heavy socks in this box, so if they're a little big, you should still be good."

Rye heard what sounded like a snicker behind him and when he glanced back, Kitt's full upper lip was caught by her ever-so-slightly crooked row of bottom teeth. When he glared at her, she compressed her lips together in a tight line, even though her blue eyes sparkled with merriment. Did he fess up and let both women know that not only did he not know how to ride, but he was intimated as hell by horses? Or did he blunder through this? Perhaps honesty was the better part of valor here. The last thing he needed was to end up on his ass in the middle of pile of horse crap and snow. "Trudy, I-I…I don't ride."

She popped out of the tack room and set the boots and socks on the step. "That's fine. Kitt, grab Jasper for Rye, right there in the third stall. Get the look of terror off your face, Rye, my big old boy is a babysitter. You'll be fine. I'll ride Penny and Kitt can hop on Laddie." She strode to the first stall and pulled out a copper-colored horse and put it between two ropes, talking a mile a minute the whole time. "This is my sweet girl. Did those mean old burglars scare you last night? Hmmm?"

His knees went weak as Kitt brought an even bigger black horse out of stall three while he shivered by the back door—frozen in fear, heat creeping up past his collar, which had suddenly gotten too tight. After she put the horse between two ropes, she looked back at him and frowned. He gave a slight shake of his head, hoping she'd get his message. *Uh-uh, no ma'am. Not going to ride that huge horse.*

"Why don't I meet you at the back of the field?" He cursed the quaver in his voice. "I'll drive around on the road and then up beside the railroad track to the gate."

"You'll get stuck. There's too much slop back there by the tracks." Trudy was tossing a pad and saddle up on the copper-colored horse. "You'll be fine on Jasper."

Kitt eyed him for a minute. "Hey, Trudy, will Jasper ride double?"

Trudy tightened the strap on the flat saddle. "Oh, yeah. My grandgirlies ride him together bareback all the time. Like I said, he's a babysitter."

"Think Rye and I could ride double out to the field if we go bareback?"

"Sure, fine with me." She tossed Kitt a brush. "I wouldn't bother putting a blanket on him, though, it'll just slip around. His body heat will keep you both warm. Here's a bridle for him. He uses a hackamore because his mouth is kinda tender since he's a senior."

Kitt brushed the horse down while Rye did all he could to calm his stomach, which was currently in his throat. She bridled the horse and he sat on the steps to pull on the socks and old boots, wondering the whole time what had happened to his common sense. He swallowed hard when she waved him over. "This is Jasper. Approach him from the side, so he can see you. You never walk directly in front of or directly behind a horse. Now, blow gently into his nose so he knows who you are, tell him hello, and rub his neck a little."

The horse's ears were about the same height as Rye himself, but he walked slowly toward the creature and did as he was told, his voice coming out huskier than normal with the greeting. "Good morning, Jasper. You're not going to buck me off, right?"

The breath Jasper returned was warm and sweet, like molasses. His brown eyes were placid and long-lashed and his black hair silky soft. The horse nickered quietly. Rye hoped against hope that Jasper was telling him everything would be fine.

"He's a Tennessee Walking horse so his gait will be easy for us." Kitt led the horse over to a wooden tack box. "I'm going to hold him while you grab some of his mane, right there"—she showed him a hank of curly black hair—"then put your leg over his back, sit, and leave me enough room to get in front of you, okay?"

Rye took a deep breath. "Okay."

She'd bewitched him. He'd truly taken leave of what sense he had left in the presence of this delectable woman. He was getting on a horse for the first time in his life, bareback. His heart pounding, he gripped Jasper's mane.

"It's going to be fine." She patted his arm. "Jasper and I will take care of you."

She meant it. She was rescuing him from embarrassment without irony or mockery. She'd simply figured out a way to help him examine the crime scene. He could do this.

Surprised by how easily he hopped onto Jasper's back, he was even more shocked by the fact that the horse didn't move a muscle as he settled down there. The horse's smooth coat heated his legs and butt like he was sitting on a fuzzy blanket.

Reins in her hand and swinging her long leg over Jasper's neck, Kitt slipped in front of him, "Okay, now scooch a little closer and put your arms around my waist. If you want to reach for some of his mane, you can, but don't pull on him, or you can just hold on to me. Try to keep your legs a little loose. Don't grip him because I'm going to give him signals with my legs. Can you relax?"

Rye surprised himself again. "I'm good," he said, and he

was.

Pressed up against Kitt's warm, straight back, he inhaled the citrus scent of her shampoo, which, combined with the clean animal odor of Jasper's coat, was oddly soothing. The poufy yarn ball on the top of her knit hat tickled his nose, so he moved his face to the side of her head.

When she turned to peer at him over her shoulder, her lush lips were mere inches from his. His heart stuttered. Of course, he couldn't kiss her. But, man, it was tempting, and when neither of them backed away, the sapphire sparkle in her eyes told him she was tempted, too.

Trudy rode past them, her brow quirked. "I'll lead."

Rye blinked. The moment was gone. However, it had been there, sure as he was sitting on the back of a damn horse; and no question, Kitt had felt it, too. The thought warmed him all the way to his toes and back again. He smiled as she chirped at Jasper to move out. "Trudy, try to avoid the tire tracks, okay?" he called. "Just follow alongside them if you can." He tightened his arms around Kitt's waist and whispered in her ear, "Let's do this."

Chapter Ten

ONCE AGAIN, RYKER forced his focus from Kitt's warm curves to the crime scene in front of and below him. Whoever had broken into and burgled Trudy's tack room had indeed come in through the back of her property. The pasture gate hung open over the muddy path along the row of tall poplars that hid the railroad track, and the path itself was a mess of deep tire imprints. Clearly, the thieves had gotten stuck a couple of times—apparently, they didn't realize that duallys are notoriously bad in mud and snow. The jerks should have been smarter and driven a four-wheel-drive truck with single tires.

From the back of the horse, he snapped a few quick pictures with his phone, then texted them, one-handed, to Duane back at the station house. He kept his other arm around Kitt's slim waist, although he'd had no problem balancing on the horse. In fact, the ride had been almost enjoyable, due more to being cuddled up against this particular beautiful woman than the novelty of being on a horse for the first time. He didn't want it to end, so, even though he had plenty of shots, he encouraged her to walk along the pasture fence, taking a few more pictures of the muddy tire tracks on the other side as they rode along.

Except for a worn leather bridle that one enterprising thief had snapped around the gate to hold it open, there wasn't a sign of any of the goods taken from the barn. After an okay from Rye, Trudy hopped off Penny to loosen the bridle before pulling the gate closed and securing it. "Is it okay to let the horses out here today?" she asked as she mounted back up with an agility Rye envied in a woman old enough to be his mother.

He tightened his hold on Kitt. "Sure. I have everything I need. I'll send somebody out to dust for prints in the tack room. Frankly, though, cold as it is, they probably wore gloves, so I doubt we'll get anything. I can stick some tape across the door to remind you to stay out of there until they're done." He gazed around Kitt's head at the path behind the fence. "I'm going to check the DMV for duallys registered around here and see what comes up."

Kitt turned her face toward him, again nearly brushing his lips with hers in the process. A bolt of lightning streaked through him. On a swift intake of breath, she tipped her head away and her voice quavered when she asked, "Do you think it could be someone from around here?"

"Possibly." Fact was, a memo had come across his desk a couple of weeks ago reporting that a couple of other barns in the surrounding counties had been burglarized. One of the victims had gotten some of his belongings back when he discovered them up for sale at a livestock auction south of Indy. He'd marked every item with his initials. "Hey,

Trudy," he called, "is your stuff marked in any way?"

Kitt nudged Jasper into what she'd described as "his gait" as Trudy slowed her horse and waited for them to catch up to her. The horse's even moves were as easy to ride as sitting on a cloud, not at all like the rough trot he'd seen in movies and on TV, although he'd have been happy at a dead run if it meant clinging to Kitt's luscious curves. They slowed to a walk when they got closer to the barn, ambling alongside Trudy.

"Everything has a number burned into the leather and I have an inventory on my computer of each item in that tack room, right down to the box of rags and bottles of fly spray."

That news didn't surprise Rye at all. Trudy Morrow was a phenom of organization, as she proved every spring running the Redbud Festival with all the panache of a commanding general. When they got into the barn, she stayed up on Penny. "I'll ride up to the house and get the latest printout for you."

Kitt rode Jasper up next to his stall. "Think you can hop off?"

Suddenly, the distance to the ground seemed way farther than it had when he'd had his arms around her out in the field. When his focus had been divided between the damage the thieves had done to Trudy's pasture and the sweet citrus scent of Kitt's shampoo, he hadn't noticed how high up he was. "Um, sure." He gazed down at the rubber-matted floor. "You want to get down first?"

She gave him a smile over her shoulder. "Nope. You're in back. I'd end up kicking you in the head if I dismount first."

Scooching forward on Jasper's neck, she held out one hand. "Here, scoot back on his butt, grab my hand, pull your right leg over, and slide down. Don't kick me."

He hesitated for a few more seconds, screwing up his courage.

"Look, Lieutenant, the floor is rubber. If you fall on your arse, the worst that can happen is you'll bounce right back up again." She chuckled, but there wasn't a moment of meanness in her warm gaze. "And maybe you'll get a bit o' horse hair on your nice clean trousers, which probably have dirt on the seat by now anyway. We'll dust you off, I promise."

"You offering to pat down my butt, Ms. Boynton?" With a determined breath, Rye reached for her hand, brought his leg between them over Jasper's wide back, and slid off, landing gracefully on his feet. However, he didn't release her hand. Instead, he tugged on it gently then caught her in his arms as she hopped off the horse. "That's the best offer I've gotten since you sashayed a straight line for me in the post office parking lot."

He held her loosely as he grinned, giving her plenty of opportunity to slip to the side. She didn't. Rather, she stood in the circle of his arms, Jasper's reins in one hand and the other clutching Rye's shoulder. Her teeth worried her lower lip as she gazed into his face, her expression unreadable. Heart pounding, mouth dry, he licked his lips. He was playing with fire, but he couldn't pull his eyes from her face or drop his arms. Couldn't—no, *wouldn't*—let the moment end.

Kitt closed her eyes, then opened them again just as quickly. "You're flirting."

"I know." His response was raspy.

"What am I supposed to do when you look at me like that?" She dropped the reins and put her other hand against his chest. Jasper stood there, perfectly still, trapping the two of them between his big warm body and the stall.

Rye shivered when she put one gloved hand on his cheek, and he struggled not to turn his face and press his lips to her leather-encased palm. He'd never been so enamored of a woman in his life. The attraction was fierce, visceral, a longing to know her that swept through him every single time they encountered one another. "Back at you, Irish," he whispered, covering her hand with his.

She had elegant hands with long fingers he was hungry to kiss, maybe even draw the tips of them into his mouth. She was so close, he could taste her breath—oranges and coffee and something else sweet. She hadn't moved away from him, but now she was gripping the front of his parka. "Do you think this is wise, Lieutenant? I mean, the whole town is betting on us and…" She let her words trail off as she wet her lips.

He wasn't sure which of them was actually trembling—one of them was or maybe both. Who knew? "Probably not. It has catastrophe written all over it, but here's the thing"—this time he *did* turn his head and kiss her palm—"I just… I can't… Oh, dammit, Kathleen…"

Her gaze drifted between his eyes and his lips and when she tipped her head, curiosity shining in her blue eyes, he gave up resisting and kissed her.

THE KISS WAS everything Kitt had fantasized about Ryker Lange since that first morning when he'd peered into her car window. Easy and gentle at first, then building in urgency until she was drowning in his lips, his arm around her, his gloved hand holding her head steady as he ravaged her mouth. How could she not respond? All in all, it was a remarkable kiss. His lips were soft; their tongues tangled in a thrust-and-parry that left her breathless. When he finally lifted his mouth, the hunger in his stormy eyes made her toes curl inside her riding boots.

Dear God in heaven, how I want him.

He rested his forehead against hers, his breathing uneven, and it was impossible to tell whether it was his heart or hers she felt thumping through the of the layers of clothing between them. A flurry of expressions chased across his face before settling on a quiet upturn of his lips, a contradiction of arrogance and vulnerability that disarmed her completely.

"Oh, God, and ye can kiss, too." She gasped when she realized she'd said the words out loud and, fingers splayed against his parka, she pushed away from him. "Why are you deliberately making yourself more attractive to me? How is *that* fair?"

"Um…excuse me?" And there was Trudy, leading Penny into the barn.

Kitt moaned inwardly. Who knew how much Trudy had

seen, heard. Straightening her shoulders, she turned away from Ryker. "I'm going to clean stalls, okay? I miss holding a manure fork. See you around, Lieutenant." She gave him a wide berth as she led Jasper down to the crossties and began removing his hackamore, replacing it with the bright blue canvas halter hanging on his stall door. When she clipped him into the ties, she caught a glimpse of Ryker, standing right where she'd left him, confusion clear on his handsome face.

"Here's that printout, Rye." Trudy had stuck Penny in her stall and picked up the wheelbarrow, shoving it down to the stall Kitt was cleaning.

Kitt could see Ryker through the open stall door, his jaw rigid, still standing right where she'd left him, staring at the paper Trudy had given him. She turned her back and shoved the manure fork into the shavings, shaking it to reveal the horse apples Jasper had left overnight. The work and the mellow odor wafting from the stall floor eased her trembling slightly. But he was still out there. She needed him to go so she could think clearly again.

"Rye?" Trudy's voice echoed in the cavernous barn.

"Um, yeah…thanks for this. I-I'll add it to my report and get one of the guys to check out auction houses around the area. You…you might put the word out to your horse friends. Let them know what happened here." Kitt could hear the quiver in his voice. *Well, good. He's as flustered as I am.* A long silence ensued, then Rye cleared his throat. "Um, Trudy, what you saw here…I mean…you know…between Kitt and me…"

Trudy laughed. "Hey, I didn't see a damn thing. And if you work hard to find my saddles, nobody at Hutchins House ever has to know you were kissing the face off your *buddy* over there."

Kitt twisted around in time to see the older woman grin and give Rye a pat on the shoulder.

"Fine. I'll keep you posted." Rye shook his head and walked out, leaving Kitt a confused mess of empty and elated all at the same time.

She went back to shoveling horse crap, starting when she felt a movement behind her. Trudy leaned against the open stall door, arms crossed over her bosom, her tiny athletic body relaxed, one foot resting on the wheelbarrow handle. She didn't speak, merely watched as Kitt sifted wood shavings and raked the floor of Jasper's stall.

After a few beats, Kitt couldn't stand it another second and she swung around. "What?"

Trudy's neutral expression didn't change, except that she raised one brow. "What?"

"What do ye want to say? I can tell you're burstin' with it."

Trudy merely shrugged. "Actually, I did have a speech going, but instead, I'm only going to say, you two are completely clueless."

Kitt's shoulders slumped as she pressed her head against the wooden handle of the manure fork and squinched her eyes shut for a few seconds. "I didn't come to America to fall in love the second I landed. Truthfully, and this may be more than you ever wanted to know about me, I came to get away from men. Well, *a* man." She smoothed the back of the rake over the sawdust. "He was a…a player, like the lieutenant. He broke my heart. I won't go there again. I can't."

"I think this stall is done, Kitt." Trudy gently took the manure fork out of Kitt's hands, laid it on the wheelbarrow, and pushed the cart out of the stall. "Jasper's never had such a tidy floor." She winked. "Go get him."

Kitt led the old gelding back into his stall and gave him a hug and a slice of carrot from the bag she'd stuck in her pocket before she left home. After she latched the sliding door, Trudy took her by the arm and gently pushed her down on Jasper's tack box, then sat across from her on Laddie's trunk. "I'm no expert on love, God knows. Todd and I just sort of exist here together. If it weren't for the horses, well, and the fact that this place belongs to *me*, I'd have left long ago. It's been in my family since my great-grandfather built it back around the turn of the century—it's my *home*. But how I'd love to be madly in love… I've never really had that in my life."

"Weren't you and Todd in love once?" Kitt wasn't entirely comfortable asking that of a virtual stranger, although Trudy had started the conversation, so it seemed rude not to go with it.

"I think Todd was in love with money and I had it. I was young and stupid and in love with love." She blew a breath into the blond bangs that showed beneath her knit cap. "He's never looked at me the way Rye looks at you—not even on our wedding day. Don't turn your back on that. It's a rare thing." She clasped her gloved hands in front of her.

"Your cousins sure found it—Sam and Conor warm my heart every time they bring Ali out to ride old Bucky over there." She nodded toward the stall next to Jasper's where a buckskin pony nickered when he heard his name mentioned. "All four of the Flaherty boys found it, but not everyone is so blessed. You need to let go and see what happens. Both of you do—forget this stupid bet."

Even though Kitt blinked back the tears that stung her eyes at the wistfulness in Trudy's words, she knew better. Guys like Ryker Lange didn't know the difference between love and lust, even if they were fine upstanding citizens who loved their community and took care of their moms and played big brother to fatherless kids. After all, look at Ethan—the *perfect family man*. Except that he wasn't because he was cheating…with her.

"Love is just lust all dressed up in a tux and a bow tie." Even as she said the words, a tinge of doubt crept in.

Ryker *wasn't* Ethan Craine. Hadn't she'd already seen that in his warm, open smile? His honest, intelligent eyes? His concern for the twins? Would a selfish bastard take the time to help two young boys? Her own heart ached, yearning for…what? A man she could trust not to destroy her, and something in Ryker Lange's kiss told her he could be trusted. Inwardly, she cursed the fear that held her back, cursed Ethan Craine for making her think her judgment was lacking somehow, and cursed Ryker Lange for being such an extraordinary kisser.

Trudy chortled and stamped her feet. "Where did you get that nugget of fortune cookie wisdom?"

"It's my own." Kitt rose, picked up the handles of the wheelbarrow, and shoved it to Laddie's stall. "I'm going to keep cleaning, okay? I need to think and my da says scooping horse crap is the best therapy there is."

"I can't argue with that, and I never turn down someone willing to pick out my stalls." Trudy shook her head and rose to lead Laddie into the aisle and crosstie him. "I'm going to go call my insurance company; I'll be back out in a few." She ran a hand over Laddie's broad flank, and although her expression was warm and her eyes twinkled, her words were deadly serious. "Think carefully, Kitt. You're too young to shut the door to your heart. Besides, sometimes the best thing in life comes disguised as a royal pain in the butt."

Chapter Eleven

K ITT TOSSED ANOTHER string of pink twinkle lights into the overloaded cart and tweaked little Maggie Flaherty's nose. The baby giggled and reached for Kitt's scarf, so Kitt unwound it and handed it to the little girl perched in the seat of the cart.

Tierney, Maggie's mom, who had been examining a display of heart-shaped crepe paper streamers, chuckled. "Oh, don't give her that! You'll so regret it. She's teething like mad so it's going to be soaked with drool when you get it back."

"But look at how happy it's making her." Kitt touched her forehead to Maggie's soft dark hair and crooned, "It's so soft, isn't it, sweet pea? Yes, it is." She rubbed the scarf on Maggie's cheek. "It's warm and fuzzy for my little cuzzy." She held up a hand to keep Tierney from dropping the package in the cart. "I think we're covered here. We've got enough stuff to decorate the entire town square. Let's go pay, then lunch is on me if you can tell me a great place to eat in this town."

"Why is lunch on you?" Tierney replaced the streamers with a regretful little smile.

"It's my policy; you drive, I buy lunch." Kitt got in line to pay with Tierney on her heels. "My sisters and I always do it that way when we go up to Dublin or Cork City. Lunch covers petrol." She began loading her purchases onto the conveyer belt. "'Twas grand of you to bring me."

Tierney waved away her thanks. "My pleasure. I needed to come to Cincy anyway and hit the Carter's sale, so it's a win for both of us." She winked. "Plus, as delightful company as Maggie is, a little *grown-up* girl time is a treat for me. Over lunch, you're filling me in on how this wager is going with our delicious police lieutenant."

KITT SMILED UP at the server as the enticing scent of chicken potpie wafted up from the plate he set in front of her. "That smells as delicious as me ma's chicken pie."

The handsome server grinned. "Are you from England?" Was everyone in America good-looking and friendly? Sure seemed like it.

"I've just come from Ireland."

"Well, cool. Welcome to America."

"Thank you. I'm having a fine time here." Kitt returned his smile, amazed once again at how perfect his teeth were and how easy and comfortable he seemed as he set Tierney's burger and fries down, along with a dish of applesauce for Maggie. Tierney also had a couple of squeezy pouches of baby food that she'd already handed to Maggie, and some tiny crackers that the kid seemed to really enjoy.

"Okay, dish," Tierney commanded, after they'd dug into their lunches. "I want to hear everything from the horse's mouth. Bren is so useless when it comes to town news. He just goes through life in his own little world." The words were said such affection that Kitt could feel the joy emanating from Tee and Bren's marriage. Seeing him so happy warmed her heart—Brendan was the Flaherty cousin she was closest to since he'd been to Ireland more often than the others. He'd spent several years in London at graduate school and came to the farm frequently during that time, pitching in with the work in exchange for learning to ride. Whenever he traveled anywhere in Britain for his job, he made it a point to spend a night or two with the Boyntons. Kitt had always come down from Dublin to spend time with him when he visited, although they hadn't seen him since the surprising news of his marriage and fatherhood.

"First tell me about you and Bren. It's been amazing to meet all the cousins' wives, but I've hardly had a chance to get to know any of ye personally."

"The guys did sort of toss you into the deep end of the winery business, didn't they?" Tierney fed Maggie another spoonful of applesauce. "Bren's told me all about the horse farm in Ireland. Man, he *loves* it there. We're hoping to go over when Maggie gets a little older."

"Oh, ye should go soon. Ma loves the wee ones. She'd be in heaven lookin' after this sweet thing." Kitt handed Maggie an oyster cracker, chuckling when the baby gripped her finger with a messy hand. "How did you and Bren meet?"

Tierney shrugged. "We've known each other since we

were kids. It was inevitable, I think. I'm so crazy about him, my only regret is that it took me so long to figure it out."

"Makin' up for lost time, are ye?"

"Most definitely."

The joy in Tierney's expression was enviable and Kitt was no stranger to that particular brand of envy. Every time Declan gazed at Maeve with his heart in his eyes, a sharp twinge of jealousy arced through Kitt, despite the fact that she was beyond delighted for her sister's happiness. How she wanted that. But somehow, she was always drawn to men who weren't capable of that kind of devotion. She smiled at Tee, while at the same time laughing grimly at herself inwardly because, despite all her best efforts, once again she was falling for a player.

Even though she hadn't seen him for a few days, Ryker's image materialized in her mind immediately—his rugged, surfer-boy good looks would set any woman's heart pounding. However, the picture that appeared in her head included young Caleb and the look of adoration on the boy's face when Rye had high-fived him for catching a nice-sized crappie. The same look was on Ethan Craine's daughters' faces when she saw them in the café in Trinity. So there was that—how do you learn to believe what is real? How do you trust what you see? "How do you know?"

"How do I know what?" Tee glanced up from finishing her burger.

Kitt snapped back to the restaurant that overlooked the gray and choppy Ohio River. "Huh?"

"You said, 'How do you know?'"

Heat rose in Kitt's cheeks. Now she was talking out loud to herself when she was supposed to be having a conversation with her lunch companion. Holy Mary, she was losing it and it was all Ryker Lange's fault. He'd taken up residence in her head and he wasn't paying rent, something Maeve had warned her against when she first started seeing Ethan. It was happening again. "I'm sorry, Tierney, my brain is just…I dunno…cockeyed, I guess."

Tee wiped her mouth and handed little Maggie a piece of a French fry, grinning when the baby practically moaned in delight. "Don't tell Bren I gave her this, okay? He's deter-mined to keep her diet *clean*, whatever that means." She leaned in and lowered her voice. "This kid eats mashed-up avocado… I'm dead serious. Sometimes, I've got to give her something *normal*, you know?"

Kitt laughed. "That is *so* Bren! Don't worry, your secret's safe with me. A bit o' pommes frites won't hurt her."

Tierney winked and nodded with another beautiful grin. "What were you asking? How do I know *what*?"

Kitt bit her lip for a moment, considering whether to plunge ahead or keep her own counsel. But Tee's open, friendly expression invited the kind of confidences she'd have shared with her sister if she were in Ireland. In fact, Tee sorta reminded Kitt of Maeve with her nutmeg-colored hair and her warm, approachable manner. She took a deep breath. "How do you know when it's…*right*? When it's true? And you're not simply fallin' for a line of cow shite? And does it smack you over the head or does it happen gradually? Which way is real?" Kitt's voice rose and she closed her lips in a tight line to keep from wailing the next question. Instead, she simply gazed at Tierney's shocked face and blinked back the tears pressing against her eyelids.

Tee reached out to cover Kitt's hand with hers. "Oh, honey. That's a question for the ages, isn't it?"

"Aye." Even though Kitt scraped the last of the potpie onto her fork, she couldn't make herself eat it as Tierney continued to stare at her, clearly considering the questions laid before her.

"I think it's a *heart* knowing," she said finally, touching her other hand to her chest. "Although Bren has always been in my heart, the first time he kissed me, I mean, *really* kissed me, I knew. He was the one. I felt that kiss all the way to my toes. I didn't admit it to myself at the time." She let out a little laugh. "And definitely not to him, but I knew."

"Remember the old, old song? 'It's in His Kiss'?" Kitt's thoughts shot to the mind-blowing kiss Rye had given her in Trudy's barn and she shivered. That kiss was…extraordinary. Touching her fingers to her mouth, she still felt his lips on hers, his fingers on the back of her head, holding her to him. She wanted more. And that yearning was like nothing she'd ever felt before.

"It was for me." Tierney wiped Maggie's rosebud mouth and tiny fingers before she turned back to Kitt, her gaze filled with curiosity, but when she took a breath to speak, Kitt shoved the plate away and signaled to the server for their check.

"You ready to go?" she asked, avoiding her new friend's piercing gaze. "I need to get back to the winery. I promised

Sean and Conor we'd go over the details of the Winemaker's Table so Mac can start planning the menu."

Tierney busied herself repacking the diaper bag, then stopped. "Hey, wait a minute. We never got around to talking about the bet." She narrowed her eyes. "Or maybe we did?"

Kitt merely looked down as she dug her wallet out of her bag. "Maybe," she mumbled.

"OKAY, MAX, I think we've got it." Rye gave the wrench on the hose connector one more quarter turn. "Tell Beck to try the water." He was freezing his butt off, lying on the ground under his mom's mobile home. The one he and his brothers had grown up in. The mobile his mother refused to give up, in spite of all three of her sons pleading with her to find a place in town.

River Run Mobile Home Park had changed a lot since the Langes had grown up there. New owners several years ago had cleaned up the park, installed lighting, and paved the roads. They'd evicted the people who hadn't paid lot rent in ages, gotten rid of the older junkier trailers, and set up neighborhood rules that everyone was expected to follow. So, okay, it wasn't what it was when he was a kid. The place where, if you lived there, other kids would either taunt you to tears or shake their heads in pity. But it was still... Oh hell, it was still the other side of the tracks in River's Edge. Old-timers often looked askance if your address was a numbered lot in River Run.

Ryker had begged his mom to come and live with him when he bought his house on Cedar Cliff Road—he had plenty of room. Jane had demurred, saying River Run was her home. When Becker came back from Indy, he'd stayed with Rye for a couple of months until he took over Tierney Flaherty's apartment in the old Victorian not far from the fire station. He'd also invited their mother to live with him, but she said there were too many steps and besides, River Run was her home. When Max finished his residency and finally moved away from the crowded apartment he'd shared with three other residents into his own loft at the Box Factory, the newly renovated warehouse down near the Warner mansion, *he* even asked her to join him there. Again, she'd declined.

Last fall, when the brothers offered to go in together to move her into a half a duplex that had come available down the street from Ryker, Jane had put her foot down firmly. Her mobile sat at the back of the park among a stand of pines and, according to her, had a better view of the river than anyplace else in town. Her friends lived nearby, and they drove their golf carts to each other's *cottages*, as they referred to them, for iced tea or wine in the summer and hot chocolate and cards in the winter. Heaven forbid anyone refer to their mobiles as "trailers" or River Run as a "trailer park." It wasn't a trailer park, it was a *neighborhood*, and it was Jane's home.

This morning, all three sons were there because the heat tape had failed on one of the water lines and a connection had burst in the freezing weather. Ryker was flat on his back on a cut-up cardboard box on top of a skim of ice fixing the broken line. Max had just returned from the farm store up on the highway with enough rolls of new heat tape to redo every damn pipe under the mobile, and Becker was in the house, trying again to convince Jane to sell out and move to town. Rye could hear the conversation through the floor and it sure didn't sound like Beck was having any better luck with that cause than usual.

Max stooped down and leaned into the cobwebby space behind the skirting. "Hey, bro, at least it's too cold for spiders, eh? Remember two years ago when that spider dropped on my face and I damn near swallowed the sucker?" He shuddered.

Rye grinned at him. "Get under here, you big chicken, and help me rewrap these lines and pipes. Since you bought so much tape, we may as well replace it all as long as we're under here."

Max looked dubious. "You really want to do that *now*? I mean…it smells like Mom's making bacon in there, which probably means waffles, too, and I haven't had any breakfast yet."

"None of us have. We've all been here since the butt crack of dawn." The tantalizing odor of the bacon he was certain was sizzling in his mother's big old iron skillet made his mouth water. Beck had probably already nabbed a slice or two. Plus it *was* damn cold and his fingers were getting stiff inside his insulated work gloves because they'd gotten wet when he'd worked on the water line. He sighed. "Okay, let's go get some breakfast, but afterward, one of you is going to help me rewrap these lines."

Max's gray eyes lit up. "Roll outta there and go get some breakfast. I'll close up the skirting so things will stay halfway warm until after we eat."

Rye's glasses fogged up as soon as he stepped inside the mobile. He set them lower on his nose as he removed his hat, gloves, scarf, and winter jacket. He usually wore contacts, but the panicked call from Jane came so early, he hadn't bothered with them. The glasses cleared by the time he'd pulled off his lace-up flannel-lined boots, so, happily, he could see the waffle iron on the counter in the kitchen. There was nothing better than his mom's waffles with melted butter and warm maple syrup.

She gave a little screech when he sauntered over to put his icy cheek next to hers. "Good Lord, Ryker Lee, you're freezing. Becker, pour your brother a cup of coffee." She opened the waffle maker to reveal a golden-brown crispy treat. Plopping it onto a plate from the stack next to her, she handed it to him. "Here, get started on this. The bacon's on the table."

Rye planted a kiss on her cheek and accepted the plate, nabbing the cup of coffee as he passed by Beck, and settled into a seat at the old wooden table. Jane's kitchen was cozy, no question about that, and full of fond memories of the four of them sharing meals as he grew up. In spite of the stigma of always feeling like an outsider, Rye's best child-hood moments had happened right here when he and his brothers and his mom had gathered for delicious meals and to rehash their days.

Jane's first question at supper each evening had always been about how their day had gone, giving each boy a chance to talk. Her cardinal rule was that they tell one good thing that happened for every complaint. Rye learned quickly to keep his list of bad things brief because otherwise he had to invent the good stuff. School wasn't a pleasant place for the Lange brothers, even though each of them had discovered a way to overcome the ignominy of where they'd grown up. Becker was a star of the basketball team and fast friends with popular Sean Flaherty, who played center all four years he was in high school. Rye was the best pitcher the River's Edge High School had ever seen and his fastball provided him a full ride to Purdue. Max was the brainy one—valedictorian of his class with scholarships and fellowships that took him right to med school.

As the others joined him at the table, Rye remembered and got that hollow in the pit of his stomach for the way the three of them had always had to try harder. How they always had to overcome what people in town believed they were simply because of where they lived. Rye blamed their father, the long-absent Donald Lange, who had dropped in and out of their young lives for years, making big promises he never kept, charming Jane into giving him money and a warm bed before disappearing again. He'd return with vows to change his womanizing ways, find a real job, and quit drinking only to vanish again when the mood struck him. The last time he'd turned up, ten years ago, the boys had formed a protective circle around their mother, while she handed Don the divorce papers that had been sitting on her desk for almost a year and sent him on his way.

Rye couldn't forget the deep feeling of pride that seeing her hand Donald those papers had given him or how he'd relished the moment she'd pointed to the door and ordered him out of *her* house. The only thing that stopped him from raising his foot and kicking the old bastard down the wide deck steps was the knowledge that he would disappoint Jane if he did. He sure wanted to, though. Even today, as he looked around at his family, the fear that Don might appear again niggled at the back of his mind.

"Dude, hey…pass me the syrup." Becker's voice brought Rye to the present and he handed his brother the pitcher. "Where are you, man?"

"I know where he is." Max chortled. "Fighting to keep his side of that bet with the Flahertys' hot cousin."

Rye simply gave him the stink eye and kept eating. There was no way he was going to get into that particular jumble of emotions with his brothers. Not while he was enjoying Jane's delicious breakfast. Besides, he wasn't convinced either of them would have any good words of advice. Becker was newly off a contentious divorce that had left him bitter about women in general, and Max was so busy at the hospital, he barely had time to shower, let alone maintain any kind of relationship. He'd considered talking to Aidan about this sudden new sensation Kitt had roused in him, but he didn't want any confessions to get back to her in passing at a Flaherty family dinner or something, so he'd kept his counsel.

"What's going on with Kitt?" Jane got up for the coffeepot and warmed up all four cups on the table. "She seems like a sweet girl. Are you two dating? How'd I miss that?"

"We're not dating." Rye reached for more bacon.

Max chuckled while Beck simply rolled his eyes. "They're doing the exact opposite of dating, Mom."

"What on earth is the opposite of dating?" Jane mopped up syrup with her last bite of waffle. "Is there such a thing?"

Rye scowled at Max, then sighed. "She challenged me to be just friends, no flirting, no dating. Somehow, the entire crowd at the double H got involved and it turned into a stupid bet that nobody believes I can win because apparently everyone in this town thinks I'm some kind of sleazoid player or something. It's no big deal, Mom."

"Why *anyone* would *ever* think such a thing about my little brother." Becker smirked, but tousled Rye's hair affectionately, laughing, really laughing, for the first time a long time.

It was so good to hear the sound of Beck's booming laugh again and so great to see the lines around his eyes crinkle up with amusement, Rye didn't even care that it was at his expense. He merely shook his head and reached his fork out to spear another waffle from the plate in the center of the table.

Chapter Twelve

JANE RAISED ONE dubious brow at Rye as she rinsed off the breakfast dishes he was setting on the counter for her. "Do those two know what they're doing under there?"

He chuckled. "Beck knows. He helped me put on the heat tape that's already down there, remember? In the dead of summer? It was a hundred degrees in the shade?"

She grinned and shook her hair out of her eyes. "I remember."

"Max takes orders well, so Beck can guide him, and I'll go back under in a minute. I wanna finish my coffee." He leaned his elbows on the counter, tracking his coffee mug around a bowl of oranges setting there. Mom always had fruit in that old pottery bowl, bright red apples or juicy oranges, bananas or grapes, ready for her sons to nab whenever they wanted. "Where'd this bowl come from? It's been here as long as I can remember."

She glanced up from loading the dishwasher. "Your dad brought that to me from Taos years ago when he was still driving over-the-road—it's a signed Kilborn piece. I've always treasured it."

Rye removed all the oranges to examine the scene in the bottom of the bowl—a pueblo and a faceless woman grinding corn as she sat on the stoop. He turned it over to study the signature etched in the base, but not really seeing it. "Why do you still treasure it after... you know, after the divorce and everything? Doesn't it remind you of *him*?" He couldn't help it. He was incapable of calling Donald Lange *Dad*. The son of a bitch had never spent a moment being a dad to him and his brothers.

Jane straightened slowly from stooping over the dishwasher. "It's a reminder of a good time in my life. I was deeply in love with your dad and when we were first married, things were... lovely." A small faraway smile appeared on her face and she hugged the dishtowel to her chest. "We had fun and he always brought me something from wherever he traveled when he was driving for the trucking company."

"What happened?" Rye piled oranges back in the bowl, trying, yet failing, to emulate his mom's more artistic arrangement. "I don't remember any fun, Mom."

She shook her head. "You wouldn't. That was before you came along."

Rye's heart sank. "Are *we* the reason he started drinking and fooling around?"

"Oh God, no, honey. *No*." Jane's eyes widened. "Don't ever think that!"

"Then why?" He had never asked his mother about her marriage, mostly because whenever Don Lange's name came up, he got so angry he could hardly see. And something else—a sort of nameless terror that he couldn't define would settle cold and hard in the pit of his stomach.

Jane set the last of the breakfast dishes in the machine and closed it. "I don't know," she admitted, and Rye couldn't read her expression. It was neither anger nor sadness, but more resignation that flickered across her lined and lovely face.

"You loved him so much, Mom, you kept giving him chances." Rye pushed, taking a chance she'd be willing to delve into Don's abhorrent behavior. "Was he always such a—" He combed his mind for a word that wouldn't offend her, yet still described his vision of his father's behavior. The only one that came to mind made him wince. "Player."

Jane ran water through her dishrag, wrung it out with more force that seemed necessary, and carefully wiped down the waffle iron. She rubbed methodically between each little square nub. At last, she looked up at him. "I think it was an escape for him. He wasn't commitment-phobic, although he was rather a flirt. He loved women and women loved him. When opportunity presented itself, as it so often did because he was charming and so damn good-looking, well… he rarely turned it down."

"Do you think he was messing around from day one of your marriage?"

She shrugged. "I don't know. I've tried not to wonder that. Honestly, I don't think so, not until he got laid off from the trucking company. He got lost, I think. That happened not long after I got pregnant with Max, so you were too young to remember him the way he was. Happy, fun, contented." Her smile was wan and her eyes sad for the briefest of moments, then she brightened again. "What are all these questions about? You've never seemed the least interested in your dad."

He frowned. "I didn't mean to upset you or make you sad."

Jane dropped the dishrag and reached for the coffeepot, refilling her mug and his. "You didn't, sweetie. I'm always glad to talk to you boys about anything. You know that. What's going on?"

Rye picked up the steaming mugs and carried them to the table. He pulled out a chair for his mother before adding cream to his coffee from the carton on the table and sitting down. Taking a sip of the hot brew, he was fully aware Jane was waiting for him to spill whatever it was that had set off the line of questions about his dad. He pinched the bridge of his nose, afraid to ask... but needing to know. "Mom, am I... I'm just like him, aren't I?"

She added cream to her mug, slowly stirring the liquids together until the coffee turned dark tan. She took a sip, another, and then another.

Rye swallowed hard, astonished that she hadn't immediately jumped to his defense. *Oh, crap.* Did that mean he *was* exactly like Donald Lange? A thoughtless, self-involved jerk who rode roughshod over women?

"Mom?"

Jane took a breath and looked him straight in the eye. "I think that's your choice. You don't have to be."

Rye bristled. "I never lie to any woman, Mom. I don't promise anything I'm not willing to give." He twisted the lid on the carton of half-and-half. "Every woman I've dated knows the score right up front."

Her eyes narrowed slightly. "Well, good for you. That certainly keeps your life simple and unencumbered, doesn't it?"

"What's that supposed to mean?"

"It means that when you date a woman, it has significance. It's not only about a few nights of pleasure for you; at your age, dating often means something more. It is supposed to be about learning to know one another. Seeing if you're a fit. You need to figure out *right up front* if she's looking for a life partner, not merely assume she wants a hookup."

"*I* haven't been looking for a life partner and I'm always honest about that." Rye hated that he sounded so defensive, but this conversation wasn't taking the route he was expecting.

However, his mother was on a roll. "So what? It's your actions that speak most loudly. And most especially when it comes to sex—"

Rye held up both hands to stop her. "We're *not* going to talk about my sex life, Mom."

She continued, bulldozing right over his objections, "I don't want to talk about your sex life, trust me! I only hope your reputation is grossly exaggerated. But sex, Ryker Lee? That's you sharing your most intimate self with another person. You can't charm someone into bed and simply move on once you've gotten what you want. Intimacy, *real* intimacy, doesn't work that way." Tipping her head, she gazed at him for a moment. "Come to think of it, why *aren't* you looking for a life partner?"

The conversation hadn't gone at all as he'd expected, which had left him rather dumbfounded, so Ryker ignored her last question and went for his own. "If you had to do it all over again, would you? Would you marry *him* again? Knowing what you know now?"

The expected, emphatic *no* never came. Instead, Jane pursed her lips, her brow furrowed in deep thought before she finally said, "Knowing what I know now?" She folded her hands on the table. "Absolutely."

"Really?"

"Yep. Your dad and I fell head over heels the first moment our eyes met. It was at the Redbud Festival. He was home from college for spring break, I was working in the Posey Pushers booth and he came over and bought a single yellow rose. He asked me my name, then he handed it to me and said, 'If I'm going to give a rose to the most beautiful woman on the River Walk, I should at least know her name.'" Her expression softened.

"Don went to college?" Ryker knew that wasn't what he was supposed to get from her confession; however, it was the only part for which he had an immediate response.

"Only for a year at Ball State. He ran out of money and took a job with the trucking company to earn more. Then...well, things changed and suddenly, he had a family to support and—"

"Are you saying you two got married because you were pregnant with Beck?" Rye didn't even try to hide the disbelief in his tone.

Jane frowned. "We got married because we were deeply in love. Whether or not I was pregnant at the time is purely incidental. My point is this—we had a shot at a great marriage until life got complicated, as it always does, and your dad bailed. He chose not to fight for us. He took the easy way with alcohol and other women, and I allowed it for too many years. I still loved him, but you can only put the pieces of your heart back together so many times before the edges start to get ragged, you know?" The corners of her mouth drew up in a sad little smile. "It's a choice, honey. Like most of life, love happens whether you want it to or not. Who you fall in love with may not be your choice; what you do about it always is."

Rye released a huge breath, trying to dislodge the weight that had been sitting on his chest since he realized Kitt Boynton had stolen his heart. It remained, however. "I never want to hurt anyone like he hurt you. I promised myself that from the first date I had back in eighth grade. *I'll never be like Don Lange.* Yet, here I am, apparently River's Edge's answer to…I dunno…Don Lange, I guess, and that's not who I want to be. My whole life, I've been terrified of turning into *him*." He shoved his fingers through his hair, then rested his chin in his palm. "That's why I've never taken a drink of alcohol. Why I've never made a promise to any woman. Never allowed myself to get entangled… It's so I never break a heart…like he broke yours." He took another sip of now-lukewarm coffee, hating the quiver in his voice.

"Now, your big old too-cool heart has betrayed you for the first time in your life. Is that it? About damn time." Jane laid a hand on his bicep. "And you're scared of hurting her? Kitt?"

Rye closed his eyes, leaning into the touch from a woman whose strength he'd admired his entire life. He could deny it, pretend he didn't want Kitt with every fiber of his being, but what would be the point of that? His mom knew him better than he knew himself—hadn't she just proved that? He nodded slowly, afraid if he spoke, his answer would come out tremulous.

"Then don't."

He opened his eyes and met his mother's dark gray eyes, so very like his own. "Don't pursue her?" The words stuck in his throat a little bit and he held his breath, praying, *Please, don't let* that *be her answer.*

Jane's smile was gentle as she cupped his cheek. "Don't *hurt* her." She lifted her shoulders and tilted her head in a gesture familiar and dear to him. "You have the best heart I know, Ryker Lee. Show it to her. Love her. It's your choice, you know? You get to decide whether to open yourself up to her and give it a shot. It's clear you're crazy about her."

Rye took his mom's hand and gripped it, like a lifeline. "How is it clear?"

And there was that half smile he recognized so well, the one that told him she knew exactly what he was thinking. "Well, I don't think I've ever seen you strung out like this about a girl, and you've never once asked me about your dad until now." She squeezed his fingers. "How do you not turn out exactly like him? *Choose not to.*"

"It's that easy?"

"Sure, it is."

He leaned over and kissed the top of her gray-blond head. "I love you, Mom."

"I love you, too. Oh, and, honey, I know you don't drink, but if the reason is because of your dad, don't be afraid to have a glass of wine or a beer now and then. You do *not* have alcoholism in your genetic makeup. Your father isn't an alcoholic." She shook her head firmly. "Not in the slightest. He's an escape artist and abusing alcohol is just another tool to keep him from having to take responsibility for anyone except himself."

Rye blinked. Those were the bitterest words he had ever heard his mother utter about Don Lange.

Jane took a sip of coffee and made a face. "This has gone cold. Tell me about Kitt and this bet you've gotten yourself into. What's that about?"

The coil of tension in Rye's belly eased for the first time since he'd kissed Kitt in Trudy's barn, and he chuckled. "First, can I ask *you* a question?"

"Ask me anything."

"Why haven't you ever gotten involved with anyone since you divorced Don?"

A little wash of pink colored her cheeks as she collected their mugs and rose from the table. "What makes you think I haven't?"

KITT SENSED HIS presence even before she looked up from

the menu Mac had handed her. The shiver that passed through her wasn't because of the chill that swept into the diner when he entered amid a chorus of *shut the door!* from the few other patrons who lingered over their suppers. She'd become so acutely aware of Ryker Lange in the past few days that the mere mention of his name or walking past the police station on her way to Holly's tea shop or simply spotting a cruiser drive down the street sent a rush of heat to her core. And it was all because of that kiss. That damn, delicious kiss.

His stubbled cheeks were ruddy from the winter air in spite of the striped scarf wrapped nearly to his chin and the puffer jacket he wore. His blond hair peeked out from beneath a bright blue knit Colts cap that made his smoky eyes seem almost blue in the ceiling lights. As he yanked off his cap and unwound the scarf, his gaze was immediately drawn to her, almost as if she'd willed him to find her among the others in the restaurant.

Truth be told, she had been testing her ability to send him mental messages, hoping he was thinking about her as much as she was captivated by him, and clearly he'd gotten one tonight. Their eyes met and clung, and for that brief moment, they might as well have been the only two people in the place. Heat shimmered between them and she longed to be able to go to him, throw her arms around his neck, and press her lips to his.

"Rye!" The shout brought her back to the diner and Ryker's brother Max sitting with Chaz and Bobby in a booth behind her table.

Rye loped across the diner, stopping to chat for a second

with Noah Barker and his two young grandsons, twins who reminded Kitt so much of her older brother Colm's sons, six-year-old Ronan and nine-year-old Rory, her throat tightened. Rye ruffled the boys' hair and pretended not be able to tell who was who, even though the kids were wearing different-colored shirts and fleece vests with their names embroidered on them. He gave Clyde Schwimmer a pat on the shoulder as he passed and when he came to the table where Kitt sat with Mac, Carly, Sean, and Conor—papers, iPads, plates, and mugs spread out between them—he paused and tapped Conor on the arm. "Hey, guys, how's it going?"

Conor half rose and shook Ryker's hand. "Good, good. Just going over menu ideas for Kitt's Winemaker's Table event."

Sean pointed one finger in Rye's direction while Kitt busied herself with the menu lists Mac had printed out for them. "Hey, you eat here a lot—what's your favorite dish?"

Rye chuckled. "As long as you include baguettes and truffle butter in this soiree, I'm there, although if the point is wine and food pairings, you've pretty much lost me."

Kitt burned inside when his soft gaze met hers. "He's right about the baguettes and truffle butter," she said. "It wouldn't be Mac's dinner without truffle butter."

Rye's next words surprised the heck out of her. "Maybe a Winemaker's Table is the place for me to finally learn about wine and food." Rye took two more steps and put his hand on her shoulder as he stood behind her and read aloud from the menu she held. "Hey, *this* meal sounds good! Coquilles

St. Jacques—man, I love scallops. Pot-au-feu—beef stew is always great in winter. Baguette and truffle butter—absolutely. Salade Niçoise, baked brie, and crème brûlée for dessert. Wow!" His French accent was impeccable and the translations spot-on while his touch lingered, his fingers pressing, releasing, pressing...

Kitt trembled as she forced herself to continue gripping the sheets of paper in her hand. But, oh, how she wanted to grab his hand, pull him down to her and—

"Rye, dude, if you keep your hand on that gorgeous babe for another second, we're all calling flirting and you've lost the bet." Bobby's voice interrupted her fantasy as it broke through the chatter in the diner.

Noah Barker's rough laugh rang out. "He's right, Lieutenant. Drop your hand or we're declaring Kitt the winner right here and now."

With a final squeeze, Rye released her shoulder and tossed a cocky grin to Noah and the others. "Hey, chill. Nothing to see here. Just patting a buddy on the shoulder. See?" He patted Mac, who sat next to Kitt, and then Carly, too, before he crossed to the booth where he belonged. "Shove over, Max." He raised his hand to Norma, who stood behind the counter. "Norma, m'love, you have any coffee left back there? Maybe some pie?"

With an effort, Kitt brought her attention back to the business at hand, although the connection to Rye was tangible to the point she could swear she felt his warm breath on her neck all the way from the booth behind her. "Want to go with the French dinner, guys?" Her voice came out rough and grainy, so she cleared her throat. "What do you think about the wine if we go French?"

Sean gave her a quizzical look, then with a twist of his lips, set the Four Irish Brothers Winery wine list in front of her and Mac. "I think the chard will go with the scallops, Cab Franc would work well with the pot-au-feu."

Conor's gaze went from Kitt, over her head toward Ryker, and back to Kitt again. With a small shrug, he said, "Maybe the pinot noir with the brie? That'll be a good pairing, don't you think, Mac?"

Kitt was grateful Mac was totally focused on the menu and not paying attention to the electricity sparking between her and the delicious cop, because she simply could not handle any teasing right now. Not when her heart was so twisted up and she could barely breathe knowing he was so close. She gave herself a mental slap. Back there was heartbreak, pure and simple, and she'd do well to pay attention to her common sense instead of her wayward imagination.

But that kiss… Oh, dear Lord, that kiss…

Chapter Thirteen

KITT SHOVED HER hands in her jacket pocket, gloves and all. The evening was remarkably warm for the first week of February in Indiana, but she was still chilled. Not enough to go home, though; walking the River Walk at dusk took her back to her strolls along the Liffey. The bouts of homesickness had lessened, her cousins and their wives had been so warm and welcoming; aye, the whole town had taken her in like a little lost puppy, but she still missed Ireland.

It had been a long day of doing inventory with Conor, a lot of stooping and bending and lifting that had left her with a need to stretch her legs. Although she'd agreed to meet Aidan and Bren at the double H for the game, she lingered by the river, inhaling the scents of ice and mustiness and crisp winter air. Lights glowed yellow in the windows of the Cotton Mill Inn and the wide porch that had been added during renovation had pink twinkle lights wrapped around the posts. Kitt had a hard time picturing the lovely place as the old abandoned cotton mill it had been only two years ago, even though she'd seen photographs.

Sam had said that thanks to Mayor Megan's pushing, River's Edge was becoming quite the go-to for tourists looking for small-town charm, fun shops, festivals, and good food. Kitt couldn't wait for spring and summer—Sean had showed her the town calendar and it was chock-full of fairs, festivals, and holidays all the way to next Christmas. She was anxious for her work visa to come through so she could really begin her the task of seeing how to fit Four Irish Brothers Winery into all the events. Exhilarating and daunting all at once, the new job was exactly what she'd needed to separate herself from the heartache she'd left behind in Ireland.

With the work and planning for the Valentine's Day dance pretty much wrapped up, her mind whirled with plans for the March Winemaker's Table, the Redbud Festival, opening night of the *River Queen*, and on and on. Aidan and Holly were busy with their Broadway theme for the new season, which she couldn't wait to see. Ma loved show tunes—those and old-time rock 'n' roll were the background music to Kitt's childhood.

She smiled to herself. She hadn't been able to get "The Shoop, Shoop Song (It's in His Kiss)" out of her head since that day at Trudy's barn. The tune earwormed its way into her soul every time she thought of Ryker, and *that* was nearly every moment she was awake. His effect was overwhelming. She had known how to live her new life in America before he came along. Everything was in place; she understood who she was here, or at least she thought she did. But *him*? What he stirred in her was like nothing she'd ever known before and she had no idea how to be in love like that. Especially when she was involved in a wager keeping her from exploring those powerful feelings.

Damn bet.

"Hey?" a familiar voice called behind her.

Ryker.

He caught up to her, matching his long stride to hers. "Why aren't you at the bar? Tip-off is in about ten."

Kitt's breath hitched when his arm brushed hers as they walked. "I'm not sure I'm in the mood for a game tonight. I've been enjoying walking. I think I'll walk as far as the Warner mansion and then head home for a cup of tea and one of the apricot scones I got at Paula's this morning." She wasn't about to admit she didn't think she could sit in the bar with him and not stare at him or even be tempted to reach for his hand or touch his foot with hers under a scarred table. "Why aren't you there?"

He lifted his chin toward the other end of the River Walk. "I'm headed to a basketball game at the junior high. Caleb and Josh are playing. I promised I'd be there."

She stopped since they were heading opposite directions. "Well, enjoy. Tell the boys I said hi."

He gazed out across the river. "Want to come watch them play? They'd love it."

"And ye?" The words were out before she could close her lips.

His smile was inscrutable in the gas lamps that lined the River Walk and he hesitated for a few seconds. "Aye, me, too."

The brogue was perfect, and probably the sexiest thing

she'd heard since arriving in America. A shudder of pleasure went through her when he nudged her with his elbow and tilted his head in the direction of the junior high school on Eighth Street. She resisted the urge to tuck her hand in his, and instead, kept her hands in her pockets and widened the space between them enough that she didn't brush against him while they walked. Inwardly, she cursed the night she'd made the wager.

WHETHER IT WAS the fact that she was watching a basketball game in person for the very first time or that the kids were playing their little hearts out or that she knew Caleb and Josh, but the game was more fun than watching the college teams play on TV. Everything about the evening was exciting, from the crowd of parents and students to the squeak of shoes on the shiny wooden floor and the unmistakable odor of adolescent boys playing hard. Both Caleb and Josh seemed to be good athletes, although Josh was unquestionably the stronger player and it was his three-point shot that led the Eagles to a win in overtime.

At the buzzer, Kitt and Rye both ran out onto the floor with other overjoyed fans to high-five the boys, but Josh sobered as he glanced up at the stands over Kitt's shoulder. When she turned around, she saw their mom and stepfather making their way down the bleacher steps. She tugged at Rye's sleeve. "We should go."

"You guys were awesome tonight!" Heedless of the sweat

dripping off their hair, he gave them each a quick bro-hug. "Proud of you."

"Great game, you two! You've turned me into a real Hoosier basketball fan!" Kitt gave them a thumbs-up as she backed away, delighted to see the huge smiles on Josh's and Caleb's faces. They really were such sweet kids.

"You want to grab a drink at the double H? I understand Hugh makes a mean Irish coffee." Rye grasped her elbow to keep her from getting shoved ahead as they exited the noisy, crowded gym, not releasing her when they were well out of the junior high.

The touch sent sparks through her veins and she pressed against him in spite of herself. A hot drink sounded good, and a hot drink sitting across from Ryker sounded like heaven. Mentally, she pulled herself up short. How smart was that, really?

Then the devil on her left shoulder winked. *What's wrong with an after-game drink with a mate?*

What indeed?

She turned her head to smile up at him. "Sure, a hot drink sounds wonderful!"

When he suddenly dropped his hand like her elbow had burned him, she glanced back around. There were Clyde and Gloria Schwimmer heading toward them on the other side of the wide sidewalk. Clyde had a definite smirk on his face.

"Wasn't that a great game?" Kitt enthused, stepping aside and stopping to let others pass them. "Did ye have young-sters playing tonight?"

Clyde gave Rye the side-eye. "Our grandson plays. Are

you two here on a…" He waggled his full white eyebrows and pointed one finger from Ryker to Kitt and back again.

"I saw Kyle out there, kicking butt. I thought he moved up to the high school this year." Rye did a masterful job of redirecting Clyde's attention.

Gloria tossed Clyde a warning look, then chuckled. "Nope, just eighth grade, but he's the tallest kid on the team."

Kitt made her eyes as wide as she could, hoping to keep the conversation away from what she was sure Clyde was insinuating. "The tall dark-haired one? *That* was your grandboy?"

Clyde was easily distracted. "Sure is. We're convinced he's headed for a basketball scholarship one day, just like old Rye here went to Purdue with baseball."

"You played baseball?"

Clyde hopped in before Rye could answer. "Best fastball in the history of River's Edge High. Coulda played for the majors after college if he—"

"Hadn't decided to become a cop." Rye interrupted what Kitt imagined would've been a fascinating story. How much more was she missing because of that damn wager? "We're off for a quick one at the double H. You guys wanna join us?"

"Oh, it's Kyle's big night, so hot chocolate and cookies at Karl and Liz's." Gloria slipped her gloved hand in the crook of Clyde's elbow.

As they turned away, Clyde called back to them, "Hey, while you're at the double H, check out the blackboard back in the pool room, it's pretty inter—*oof.*" He looked down at Gloria. "What'd you do that for?"

"Just say good-bye, Clyde." Gloria steered him away, taking two short steps to every one of Clyde's long strides.

Kitt's stomach tightened. "What's he talking about, Ryker?"

Rye raised one brow. "I don't know. I haven't been in there in a couple of weeks, frankly, because I've kinda been avoiding all those guys since...you know, since we made the bet. Come on, Irish, let's go take a look."

THE TAVERN WASN'T packed even though the game was still going on—Rye could hear shouts and moans coming from the back room as soon as they opened the heavy oak doors at Hutchins House. He hitched his chin toward the bar. "Want to go order for us? I'll go see what Clyde was talking about."

"Hell, no," she scoffed. "I want to see this, too."

"You know what they'll think if we show up back there together."

"They don't think you and Bobby are on a date when you come into the bar together, do they? Or you and Chaz or Jack or Aidan?" Her expression plainly said she was going to do whatever she wanted anyway, so he simply shrugged and led the way.

"Rye!" The group in the back room welcomed him raucously over the din of the TV and pool balls clacking.

"Oh, and Kitt's here, too." Bobby waved a pool cue at

Kitt as she slipped around Rye.

"Hi, Kitt." The chorus was more *Hiiiiii, Kiiiitt* with the words strung out and vowels overemphasized, which irritated the heck out of Rye, although, he managed not to give any of them the finger or even a hard stare. Instead, he eyed the TV. Kentucky was up by ten over Wisconsin in the last three minutes of the fourth quarter, and from the pile of bills in the center of the table where Eli and Jack sat, it looked as if those two Wildcats were about to clean up.

It was the blackboard on the back wall that interested Rye more, though. Some enterprising soul had made two columns with Kitt as the first header and his own name as the second. Hash marks, names, and dollar amounts indicated that at least forty-odd people had an opinion about who would crack first in this stupid flirtation wager and were willing to put money on it. Not surprisingly, Kitt had way more tally marks and names in her win column than he did in his. As a matter of fact, only about nine people thought he would win the bet.

Before he had a chance to say anything at all, the lady in question marched over to the blackboard. Straightening her shoulders and narrowing her eyes, Kitt smacked her hand against the dusty surface. "Hey!" she said, getting louder as she banged a fist on the table under the board. "Hey, you eejits!"

Chaz grabbed the remote and muted the game, while Bobby and Noah rested their pool cues on the floor and looked up at her expectantly.

"What the bloody hell is this, eh?" Kitt pointed to the

tallies and then specifically to the circled number below the hash marks. "And *this*?"

Noah chuckled. "Just a little friendly wagering, Kitt; don't worry about it. Almost everybody's got their money on you to win."

Kitt's blue eyes sparked in the dim overhead lights. "Don't worry? Are ye serious, man? You've put cash money on *me*? Like I'm some sort of damn racehorse?" She glanced at the board again. "Ryker, look at this!"

Rye stalked over to the board, his blood already boiling. If the circled figure was actually money, there was exactly $897 in a pot. "Y'all are putting *money* on whether or not Kitt and I can manage not to flirt until Valentine's Day? You guys can't possibly be *this* bored."

Chaz grinned. "Sports betting is legal in Indiana now, Rye, so don't get your panties in a bunch."

"Yeah," Andy Shea piped in. "And if you think that watching the two of you dance around each other doesn't qualify as *sport*, then you're both more gaga that any of us realize. In fact, I'm going to put another ten bucks on Kitt, buddy, because she at least has enough class not to stare at your ass when you walk by."

"Where's the money?" Rye demanded, not sure what he was going to do with that information. Maybe grab the cash, toss it across the room, and let them crawl around on the floor to sort it out.

"Hugh's holding it for us in the safe," Bobby said, picking up his cue and refocusing on the balls arranged on the green felt pool table.

Kitt stomped her foot. "This bet is between Ryker and me, you wankers! It has nothing to do with any of you. It's one thing to be followed all over town, having people watching every move we make. That's annoying as hell, but it's quite another that you've started a bloody pool!" Her cheeks had turned rosy and for a moment, her body went rigid with anger. Suddenly, though, she relaxed, and her full lips curved upward slightly. "Okay, fine. That's a tidy sum you've collected there, laddies." She pointed to the circled figure. "So I tell you what. On February fourteenth, no matter which of us wins this wager, Ryker and I will choose a charity for it."

Rye grinned so hard, his cheeks ached as groans of *no way!* and *seriously?* and *you've got to be kidding!* followed a moment of dead silence at her announcement.

Kitt grabbed the eraser from the blackboard tray and hovered it over the two columns. "That's the deal or I erase this right now and you'll never know which of you *could've* been a big winner. But just think, ye rotters. Ye'll be heroes—your special Valentine's Day gift to some deservin' charity."

Man, the woman has what Mom would call moxie!

Standing there, staring them all down, she was magnificent. If Rye hadn't already been completely nuts about her, this little scenario would have clinched it for him. With aplomb, the woman had just taken on an old boys' network that was pretty well entrenched in this town. The old-timers and the new ones aging into the traditional Tuesday game night at the double H were sometimes hardcore jokers.

Although they'd never intentionally hurt anyone, once in a while their gags went a step or two too far. Every last person in the room had been the butt of their sometimes off-color humor at one point or another. For them, it was all about how you handled them, and Kitt Boynton, the new girl in town, had just played them like a concertmaster. In spite of the unhappiness at her declaration, grudging respect showed on every single person's face.

Rye stepped closer to her. "Just erase it now, Irish, and we'll call off the bet, collect the pot from Hugh, and give it to the Tweens Club at St. Agnes."

Noah scowled and shook his pool cue at them. "No, see the damn bet through. We agree to donating the money. Hell, Rye, it's been worth it just seeing you tripping all over your own heart. We can't wait to see how this ends." He scanned the group. "Right?"

After a moment or two of grumbling and elbows in the ribs from a couple of wives and girlfriends, the others agreed, so Kitt dropped the eraser in the tray and brushed her hands together. "That's just grand now, lads. Father Mark will be so touched by your generosity."

As Chaz turned the sound back up on the TV for the last few seconds of the game, she held up her right hand and Rye blinked, realizing she meant to high-five him. He smacked her palm gently but firmly and returned her grin, satisfaction washing over him. Turning to leave, he stopped short as she wandered among the few tables, winning them all over again with a smile, a quick pat on the shoulder, or a kind word to each person.

They were in this thing together, the two of them. Whether she or anyone else in the room realized it, the wager had suddenly become him and Kitt against the world.

Chapter Fourteen

S TEPPING INTO PAULA Meadows's Bread & Butter Bakery was almost a spiritual experience—the heavenly scents of cinnamon and sugar and yeast and fruit, the scent of pastry basically, assaulted Rye's senses as soon as he opened the door. He inhaled deeply and headed for the coffee service set up on a counter near the window.

Paula's assistant, Olive Sutton, offered her usual sunny smile. "Morning, Rye."

Rye always felt a small pang when he ran into Olive— her only child, Mandy, whom Rye had graduated from high school with, had been killed in a car wreck during his first year on the force. A drunk driver had taken Mandy's young husband and her baby daughter at the same time—Olive's first and only grandchild. Ten years later, town gossip was that Olive's husband still hadn't really recovered from the tragedy and spent his days out in his woodshop, making toys for a baby who would never play with them. That the woman could even smile, let alone be chipper, amazed Rye.

Sadly, the driver was already out of prison after serving only ten years of his twenty-four-year sentence for vehicular manslaughter. Rye had been at the parole hearing and, although he fought to keep the guy in prison, his impassioned plea fell on deaf ears at the parole board. The guy did a great impression of a remorseful man who'd learned his lesson, but Rye could see the truth in his eyes. He'd be back drinking and driving as soon as Indiana reinstated his license.

"Hello, Olive, your gorgeous smile is exactly what I need on this cold and gloomy February morning." He filled a cup with French roast and added cream.

"Happy to be of service to you, Lieutenant. If you like, I can add a bear claw or a strawberry Danish to make your morning even brighter."

"Mmmm…you wicked temptress!" He examined the glass case of goodies. "How about a bear claw?"

Olive slid open the case. "To go or on a plate?"

"On a plate. I'm going to hang out, read last night's *Evening World*, and people-watch while I eat my breakfast." He pulled out his Visa and when she raised one hand in protest, he shook his head firmly. "Listen now, I'm happy to accept free coffee, but I pay for my guilty pleasures. As a matter of fact, toss one of those sour cream cake doughnuts on there, too, and ring me up."

Carrying the plate and his coffee, he settled down at a round table by the window, vaguely aware of how incongruous his big body looked in the small café chair, and not at all concerned about it. Paula made the best damn pastries in town and he'd sit cross-legged on the sidewalk in the snow if it meant he could eat anything that came out of her kitchen.

The first thing he saw when he opened the newspaper

was a quarter-page ad for the Four Irish Brothers Winery Valentine Dance that was coming up in a few days. Below the ad, stringer Jill Williamson had written an entertaining piece that included the whole Flaherty clan, featuring an interview with Kitt, whom Jill described as "a lovely young woman newly arrived from the old country."

Rye snickered. *Wouldn't Kitt's family love to know they lived in "the old country"?*

He couldn't argue with the lovely part, though, and the article brought to light some details he didn't know about Kitt. Like the fact that she had a double degree in marketing and graphic art from University College Dublin or that she'd won numerous awards for barrel racing and other horse-related activities while she lived in Ireland or that she had six brothers and sisters and several nieces and nephews.

He peered at the paper, his eyes narrowing. Good Lord, she was an extraordinary artist, as well. According to Jill's feature piece, his Irish lass had pen-and-ink sketches of old castles and churches and public buildings around Ireland being sold in a gallery in Dublin. He reached for his phone and plugged the gallery's name into Google. A few taps later, there were Kitt's sketches clearer than in the newspaper photo, priced in euros and absolutely stunning in their intricacy. Pastry forgotten, he scrolled through the inventory—an eerie drawing of an abandoned castle, a detailed sketch of Christ Church Cathedral in Dublin, another drawing of the abandoned St. Mary's church in County Wexford, and one of the Brazen Head—according to the description, the oldest pub in Ireland. There were at least sixty others and every one of them could be purchased uncolored as shown or hand-colored by someone named Rian Boynton, whom Rye assumed was a relative of Kitt's.

He tossed the phone on top of the newspaper, thrust his fingers through his hair, and dropped his head in his hands. Dammit, this was information he should be learning from *her*, not reading it in the newspaper. This was the stuff of a first date and a second, sharing details about each other's lives over a meal at Mac's diner or while walking along the River Walk. *Stupid bet!* He'd missed discovering on his own who Kitt was because he'd fallen down the rabbit hole of that freaking wager, and now the whole town already knew how remarkable she was before he'd even had a chance to have an intimate conversation with her.

Cold struck the back of his neck, but he didn't bother to look up to see who'd entered because he was absorbed in the gallery website again, scrolling through her sketches and prints.

"You okay, Rye?" A soft voice pulled him back to the bakery and he blinked, bringing Harley Cole, one of the teachers at the Growing Tree preschool attached to St. Agnes church, into focus.

He rose. "Oh, hey, Harles. I'm fine, why?"

She lifted her chin and gave him a little smile. "You were sitting there with your head in your hands, I thought maybe you were feeling bad or something."

Brown-eyed, tall, and slender, Harley wore her long chestnut-colored hair in a ponytail that bounced when she walked and, man, her walk was a sight to see. It was jaunty and so innocently provocative that nearly every man in town had been known to stop dead in their tracks when she passed by. She was a lovely woman, smart and funny, vivacious and appealing as heck. Rye gazed at her, trying to recall why he'd stopped dating her several years ago... Kids... Was it that she wanted a family and he wasn't in that place then? He couldn't remember for sure. She was still single and had lately been seeing...who? *Oh, damn, Andy...* Hadn't he seen them at Mac's together a few times? She deserved better than handsy Andy...or him, for that matter...

"Rye?" She set her steaming to-go cup on the table next to his. "Are you sure you're okay?"

Ryker shook his head, then pointed to the chair opposite his. "Do you have time to join me for a minute? I-I need to ask you something."

She offered him a puzzled smile, glancing up at the sunflower clock above the bakery's door. "Um, sure. For a minute." She sat, placing her purse and a canvas bag Rye was sure held some sort of fun surprise for her students, on the floor next to her. She unwound the wool scarf from around her neck and took a sip of coffee. "What's up?"

He sucked in his cheeks, unsure how to word what he wanted to know. Best just to come out with it. "Harley, did I break your heart?"

Her expression transitioned from startled to bewildered to bemused all in a matter of seconds before she repeated the question. "Did you break my heart?"

Heat rose up Rye's neck and he tugged at the collar of his yellow oxford shirt. Suddenly his tie felt too tight. He closed his eyes for a second. "Never mind, that sounded way less arrogant in my head. Sorry."

Harley took another sip of coffee before resting an elbow on the table and setting her chin in her palm. "Yes," she said softly. "You broke my heart."

For an instant, Rye couldn't bear to meet her eyes. "Oh, God."

"Rye." She put a hand on his forearm. "Look at me."

He manned up and met her eyes. His moment of making amends had come and it had nothing at all to do with the wager he'd made. "I'm so sorry, Harles, so very sorry."

She made a little chuffing sound. "Listen, it was ten years ago. We were both so young. Look at me now; I'm all grown up and I'm over it. And, you know, you taught me something really important."

"What would that be? Stay away from sleazy guys like me?"

She laughed and his heart twisted a little at the memory of how her throaty laugh had always turned him on when they were dating. "No. You taught me that it's worth waiting for the real thing, even if it means you get your heart broken a little bit along the way."

His throat tightened and he swallowed the lump forming there, unsure of what to say next.

Harley made it easy for him, which was so like her. She reached over and kissed his cheek, then she picked up her coffee and her bags and stood. "You're a good guy, Ryker Lange. Don't ever doubt that. Or that you deserve to find someone you can give your heart to. You do, you know? We both do. Whoever marries you will be a very lucky lady." She started to walk away, then turned back to him at the door. "Hey, Rye? Thanks. You've restored my faith in the male of the species this morning"—she held up one hand, her thumb and index finger apart about half an inch—"just a little bit." Grinning, she shouldered the glass door open and walked out.

Rye sighed and watched as she crossed the street to St. Agnes Church and her kids. Then he got back on his phone and ordered a K.E. Boynton original—a haunting hand-colored sketch of the ruins of Dunbrody Abbey in County Wexford.

KITT BALANCED PRECARIOUSLY on the second-to-the-top step of the tall ladder, trying to reach the hook screwed into the beam above her head. Maybe she should have waited for Bren; however, he wasn't home from his poker game yet and it was already ten P.M. She only wanted to get the final string of lights hung up and head home to bed. She couldn't remember being so tired since she'd arrived in America.

The sound of a heavy tread on the deck outside surely wasn't Bren. First of all, she hadn't heard his new diesel pickup, which was loud enough to wake the dead, as Ma would've said. Besides, he'd be coming in from the cellar, not the deck. The steps drew closer, and oh, dammit, she'd forgotten to turn the sign on the door over to CLOSED. Who would think a winery was open this late anyway? Was the door locked? She thought for a moment. No, dammit, she hadn't locked it yet.

"We're closed!" she yelled, exasperated as the string of lights came off three of the hooks that she'd already placed it over. "Bren, is that you out there? Get in here. I need some help."

No answer, although whoever it was had turned the doorknob on the heavy oak door and she could see his big frame outlined in shadow in the long sidelight by the door.

"Hey, we're not open!" She shook head in disgust and started back down the ladder just as the door opened. "Excuse me, we're not—" In that instant, her foot slipped into the ladder and she teetered backward.

Oh, crap.

Her foot and then her ankle slid over the textured surface of the step and she struggled to keep her balance. The door flew the rest of the way open and those heavy footsteps sounded behind her as the ladder tilted precariously back with Kitt's jeans caught on a step and her calf scraping on the rough metal. She leaned in trying to prevent imminent disaster when she was swept away from the falling ladder and into Ryker Lange's strong arms.

He leaped back from the ladder, somehow managing to use one foot to stop it from crashing into the tasting bar. Kitt cringed and hid her face against his shoulder as the ladder rocked back and forth for a moment before settling onto four legs. He got his own balance back and took a good look at her.

"You okay?" he asked, his breath hitching on the question.

He really ought to put her down, but it felt so good to be in his arms, she wasn't about to suggest it.

"I'm fine." Her voice came out a little husky and she couldn't stop breathing him in. Cedar and musk and crisp winter air emanated from his person.

"Good." He was staring and his arms tightened when she moved slightly. His cheeks were rosy with cold and his smile revealed those perfect white teeth. His breath, redolent of coffee and something sweet and cinnamon-y, made her want to taste his lips.

Instead, she simply returned his smile. "Thanks for the rescue. Um, you can probably put me down now," she suggested, making no move to take her arms from around his neck. In fact, how had her fingers found their way into his hair? Oh God, was she really stroking the back of his neck, smoothing her fingers over his wind-tousled hair? She dropped her hand to his shoulder, her cheeks scorching hot.

"Are you sure you're not hurt?" He peered into her face, making no move to set her down.

"I'm fine, truly." It was so hard to sound normal when being so close to him literally took her breath away. *Get a grip, Kitt.* She cleared her throat. "And I imagine I'm getting a bit heavy."

"Not at all." He set her carefully on her feet anyway. "What were you doing up there?"

"Gettin' the last of the twinkle lights up for the dance on Saturday." She glanced up ruefully. "And makin' a mash of it."

He unzipped his coat, slipped out of it, and hung it over the back of a nearby stool. "Here, let me do it. After all, I'm the reason you nearly fell. Besides, I'm taller." He steadied the ladder, then climbed, scanning the beams above his head. "These four hooks? Right here?" When she nodded, he slipped the light string over the hooks. "How's that?"

"Perfect." She smoothed her hands over her hips and when his smoky stare followed her movements, she suddenly became very aware of her ratty sweater unraveling at the cuff, her hair falling into her eyes, the scruffy trainers that had a hole in the toe, and, oh damn, the stupid Paddington Bear socks. Well, it was too late to change her appearance now, so she marched to the box of decorations on the tasting bar. "What brings you up here this time of night?"

"I was dropping Bren off at his place." Carefully he backed down the ladder, agilely hopping to the wood floor from the third step. "He had a little more beer than usual at the game after telling us Tierney is pregnant again. He kept toasting with *Who da man?* until *da man* could no longer see his cards. I told him I'd come down and let you know he wasn't going to be helping you tonight." He looked around the winery. "Is there anything *I* can do to help?"

Kitt burst out laughing at the picture of her buttoned-up cousin too pissed to drive. "Bren never could keep a secret. No, you got the last of the lights up, so thanks for that. I'm pretty much done now anyway. The rest of it will have to wait until Saturday. We'll close at five and finish decorating before everyone arrives for the dance at seven thirty. I'm, uh…I'm going to hang the heart garland on the mantel and close up."

She turned away and stacked the empty light packages in a bin as the silence stretching between them edged toward uncomfortable. She was rarely ever at a loss for words, but Rye's intense scrutiny had turned her into a tongue-tied teenager. Damn him for that.

He might have been feeling the same way because, out of the blue, he blurted, "Oh, hey, Trudy managed to recover some of her tack. A friend saw her saddles at an auction up in Rushville and let the auctioneer know they were hot. They called the county sheriff, but the guys had already fled the scene by the time they got there. Probably saw the auctioneer eyeing the gear and...well, took off...you know?" He was rambling, which heartened Kitt.

"I heard. I was out helping her with barn work when she got the call." She glanced over her shoulder.

He'd moved a couple of steps closer.

When she looked up from the bin, he was standing less than a foot away.

He chuckled. "I'm sorry for scaring you. I didn't mean to," was what he said, however, his expression said something very different. Something more...intimate.

"It's okay." She yanked a foil garland of pink and red hearts out of the tub and scurried around him to the fireplace. "You rescued me from what could've been a nasty fall. Thank you." Then, holding one end of the garland up to the wide beam mantel, she muttered "Bollocks" under her breath when she realized she'd left the hammer and brads on the bar next to the bin.

"What do you need?"

She blew a frustrated breath into her bangs. "The hammer and that little box of nails, if you don't mind."

"Not at all." When he brought them to her, he stood behind her and set the box of nails on the mantel. "Here, show me where you want the brads and I'll knock them in for you."

Kitt closed her eyes for a second. His breath on her cheek sent goosebumps chasing down her arms. "Um…" She pointed to the end of the mantel. "Just here…and here…" She stepped away, holding the garland along the straight line of the fireplace, showing him how she wanted it to drape. He followed her, pounding a nail and another and then another until they reached the other side. Hands shaking, Kitt hooked the garland on the last brad. She backed up to admire the effect and made a little moue of satisfaction. "There's that done, then."

Rye came to stand beside her. "It'll look nice in the firelight on Saturday."

"Aye." When she glanced over at him, he was staring at her again in that way that made her heart pound and desire pool in her belly. "Stop it, Ryker."

"What?"

"Looking at me like that."

"Like what?"

"Like you think you're falling in love with me." She turned away and whispered, "Don't fall in love with me."

He touched her shoulder, murmuring, "Too late." Gently, he brought her back around to face him, peering into her eyes, a muscle working in his jaw. He touched her cheek and then deliberately, so very deliberately it felt as if he was moving in slow motion, he kissed her full on the lips.

A shiver of longing eddied through her—a heady, languid sensation that her brain told her was simply biology, even though her heart knew it was chemistry too strong for her to fight. She leaned into him, savoring the feeling of his lips on hers, his seeking tongue, and his hands tilting her head until they fit together perfectly.

When at last, he lifted his mouth and dropped his hands to her shoulders, they were both breathing hard and his eyes shone with anticipation in the overhead lights. "Kitt..."

She put her hands on his chest and she could feel his heart pounding in rhythm with hers. The fierceness of her desire for him frightened her with its urgency and when she spoke, her voice was strained, as though the words were being squeezed out of her. "You need to go now."

His fingers tightened on her biceps. "Wait... Will you wait? I-I..."

She shook her head, blinking back the tears burning her eyelids. "We can't. *I* can't. Not again."

He stepped back and shoved his fingers through his hair, tousling it and making him look even more attractive. "Could you please, just once, try to stop seeing that Irish bastard every time you look at me? I don't know what he did to you, but I'm *not* him, Kitt." He paced to the fireplace, then back to her, standing so close she felt the heat of him. "You know what? Screw the bet." He raised both hands imploringly. "I think we have something special here. I want to see if we can make it work. Don't you?"

"It's not about the bet." She swiped at her cheeks, determined not to break down in front of him. "It's me."

"What does that even mean it's *you*?" He reached for her again, then dropped his arms. "It's *us*, Kitt. It's what I know *we* can be if you just give us a chance."

She turned away from him. "There's no *us*, Ryker. I don't know how to be an *us*. Maybe that's something I'll never know." She eyed him for a moment. "Do *you* know how?" She hated herself for putting the question to him so coldly, her tone clearly telling him she didn't think he had a clue how to be part of an *us*.

The agonized look in his eyes nearly undid her, but the painful truth was so deeply ingrained that she didn't know how to explain her demons to him, and she was too exhausted and vulnerable to try. "Please just go."

He released a frustrated sigh and, shoulders drooping, he grabbed his jacket off the chair and walked slowly to the door. He opened it and stopped, but didn't turn to face her. "I'm going, but I'm not giving up. From the moment I met you, I knew. You're the one, Kitt. I think you know it, too."

Chapter Fifteen

KITT SCANNED HER list for the hundredth time in the last four hours. "What am I forgetting?" She gazed at the other three women grouped around her. "If something has slipped through the cracks, I want to know now, not at seven tomorrow night when guests start arriving."

Sam heaved herself up onto a barrel in the Four Irish Brothers Winery's cellar and moaned. "Argh! *Nothing!* My Lord, woman, this is the most perfectly planned event I've ever participated in. Will you chill out?"

Holly nodded as she rested against the office doorjamb. "Aidan keeps saying you'd make a fabulous stage manager for the *Queen*, and he's right. You are *relentless*."

Megan agreed with a weary nod as she leaned on the barrel Sam had appropriated. "Seriously, if the guys didn't have first dibs on you, I'd hire you as the event planner down at city hall. I've gone through no fewer than three people since I got reelected last year and I still end up doing way too much myself for town events."

"That's because you suck at delegating, wife of mine." Sean appeared in the doorway with their son, Finn, in tow and Conor and Sam's snow-suited baby, Liam, on his hip. He released his grip on Finn's hand and pointed at Holly and Meg. "And don't either one of you dare put any ideas in Kitt's head. She's ours." He tossed Kitt a wink before turning back to Meg. "Friday night family dinner is at Conor and Sam's instead of Bren's. Bren ordered pizzas because it's the only thing that doesn't make Tee want to gag. He is bringing a salad, though, Carly made brownies, and we're contributing ice cream. It's all on the table in"—he glanced at his wrist—"about thirty-seven minutes according to Bren. So close up here, ladies, and be sure to grab a couple of bottles of zin, okay?"

Kitt closed her notebook with a resigned sigh. "I'm not going to be working anywhere if my visa doesn't come through pretty soon. I'll be on a plane back to Ireland." It was the first time she'd spoken those words out loud because the very thought of leaving River's Edge made her heart ache.

"It'll come through," Sean assured her while at the same time grabbing Finn away from the nearest stainless-steel fermenter. The little boy had wrapped his fingers around the valve, which was right where he could reach it easily. "Don't even think about it, bud."

Sam held out her arms. "Here, I can take Liam, Sean."

"That's okay. I've got him. Besides he loves to sit on my lap while I drive the cart. We'll meet you down there." He tightened his hold on Finn's jacket hood. "Come on, dude. Golf cart ride."

Finn's little face lit up. "Can I ride in back?"

Sean chuckled. "Sure, if you hold on."

"I'll hold on tight, I promise. Da, did you know that velociraptors' name means swift seizer? What's swift mean? Griff says…" Finn's chipper little voice faded as they disappeared up the steps.

Meg shook her head. "Can I just say I love it that Finn gets to grow up with his cousins? He's probably going to be an only—" Her voice broke, but she blinked back the tears shimmering in her golden-brown eyes. Pressing her lips together, she finally confessed, "We used our last embryo and it didn't work. I don't know if I have it in me to do the whole process again. Harvesting eggs, doctors' appointments, and the waiting…"

Holly leaped up and she and Sam surrounded their sister-in-law, offering words of comfort as Kitt stood back, wanting to join them, but unsure whether she belonged in such an intimate moment between close friends. When Holly reached a welcoming hand out behind her, Kitt rushed forward for the group hug.

Meg swiped at her cheeks. "Dammit. I want to be done crying over this. We have Finn and he's such a joy. And even though Sean says Finn is plenty for him, I still feel like I'm failing him and—"

"Hush now." Sam stroked Meg's blond hair off her damp face. "Sean worships you and Finn. The three of you are a perfect family."

"That's right," Holly agreed. "The three musketeers."

Kitt placed a hand on Meg's shoulder. "You know, when my brother Seamus and his wife, Colleen, couldn't get pregnant again after they had Addy, my ma told them that perhaps the wee girl was destined for great things and needed *all* their attention." She shrugged. "Finn is so bright—he may the one to discover a cure for cancer or become the person who brings world peace. All because he was the focus of your and Sean's lives."

The three women eyed her for so long that Kitt wondered if she'd said something wrong until Meg threw her arms around Kitt's neck. "Thank you!" She tightened the hug for a brief second before releasing her. "I've never thought of it that way before."

Kitt smiled. "Well, Lord knows I'm the last person you'd ever want advice from about love, but I do know about families, and yours is just…brilliant."

Sam hopped off the barrel. "Let's get to the house. I can only imagine poor Tee up there with four Flaherty men and six kids, although they do have Matty to keep order."

Holly grinned. "Matty's turning out to be a world-class babysitter, isn't he? He can change a diaper in forty-two seconds flat, which beats Aidan's old record of fifty seconds." She side-eyed the others. "Yeah, it's a contest. *Men.*"

Kitt warmed herself at the Flaherty women's teasing chatter as they closed up the winery, turned out the lights, and set the alarm. How she missed her sisters. She followed the others across the gravel parking lot, and when they indicated they would see her down at Conor and Sam's, she hesitated. "You know, you guys go ahead. I'm exhausted. I think I'm going to go home, get into something cozy, and have a cup of tea and a scone."

Sam narrowed her eyes. "You okay?"

Kitt nodded. "I'm fine. I-I need some downtime."

"Well, you sure won't get that at a Flaherty Friday night dinner," Meg chortled as she opened the passenger side door of Sam's SUV. "You sure you don't want to come grab some pizza to take home?"

"No, if I go down there, I won't want to leave, and I need to be alone for a while."

Holly trotted back and gave Kitt a hug. "Go on home. The dance is all under control and you need to get some good rest before tomorrow night."

"Hey, Kitt," Meg called over the top of the car. "I meant to ask earlier, you got a date for the dance?" She waggled her perfect brows. "Sean said the diner was buzzing this morning about who won the bet. Does Rye have a date or does he have to find some brokenhearted woman to make amends to?"

Kitt shook her head, trying not to let her disappointment show. "Neither of us won. See you guys tomorrow." Hopping into the Jeep, she sent a prayer heavenward that it would start on the first crank and the heater would clear the frost off the windows fast so she wouldn't have to get out and scrape.

She hadn't seen Ryker since he'd been at the winery on Wednesday and she couldn't get his words out of her head...or her heart. *Too late.* That was what he'd said when she told him not to fall in love with her. *Too late.* Did that mean he thought he *was* in love with her? Her heart thumped faster as she remembered the electric current between them, and Ryker's kiss, hot and urgent and *so* delicious. As the car warmed up, she laid her head on the steering wheel and closed her eyes.

In spite of her enthusiastic planning, she was dreading the dance. Folks from the pub would be popping with curiosity to see how the bet turned out. Fact was, the bet felt like it had gone by the wayside because kissing certainly constituted flirting, didn't it? And so did declarations of love. *Too late.* Was it a declaration? He'd murmured it so softly. Did he even mean for her to hear it? However, he'd also dropped *you're the one* as he walked out the door.

No one had ever said that to her before. *You're the one.* She'd heard her share of sweet-talking, no question about that. How else could Ethan Craine have ever weaseled his way into her heart? Ryker's simple declaration, though— *you're the one*—nearly turned her inside out. She raised her head and swiped tears from her cheeks.

As frightening as it was to admit it, even to herself in the solitude of her own car, Ryker Lange was the man she'd been waiting for all her life. She was as sure of that as she was certain she belonged at Four Irish Brothers Winery. The knowing had been deep inside her since she'd run into him in the diner the night that she rented Mac's apartment, seeing his adorable, self-deprecating smile when he knocked everything off the counter, soaking his trousers in the process. The moment he'd turned that intrigued smile on her when she'd told him the devil was just behind him. How his smoky eyes had captured hers as he tossed the grains of salt over his shoulder. If she hadn't walked away, she would've thrown herself into his arms right there in the diner.

For all the logical reasons, she'd tried hard to convince herself it wasn't serious. He was only another player. In real life, people didn't fall in love at first sight; that was stuff of fairy stories. She'd get hurt all over again—her heart wasn't healed enough to take on a new relationship. And what would be the point if she had to leave the country if her work visa didn't come through before her travel visa expired?

She'd done a brilliant job of convincing herself and everyone else that Ryker Lange was of no romantic interest to her whatsoever. Her heart, however... Her heart knew the truth.

He's the one.

RYKER SAT AT his desk at police headquarters, trying to focus on the incident reports in front of him, even though his mind was miles away—okay, *seven* miles away at the winery, where in his imagination, he was dancing by the light of the fireplace with a certain Irish lass. Every muscle tightened as he remembered holding her in his arms and when he licked his lips, he swore he could still taste her wine-sweet breath on them three days later. He closed his eyes, picturing the open bottle on the tasting bar, but he couldn't recall the label. The glass sitting next to it had had white wine in it.

Impulsively, he googled the Flahertys' winery and clicked to their products page. The wine list had at least six whites, several with names he couldn't pronounce. He cruised the list curious to see if he could pick out the taste on Kitt's lips from the descriptions of the wines. *Sweet. Luscious. Tantalizing.* All words he would use to describe the kisses they'd shared that night. Other words—*oaky, fruit forward, medium-bodied*—left him intrigued, while *toasty nose* made him laugh out load. What the hell was a toasty nose? And did Kitt know all the wine terms and what they meant?

He picked up his phone and pulled up his contacts, scrolling to her name, debating whether texting her would make her pissed off at Bren, who'd given him her number in exchange for driving him home the night of the poker game. He put the phone back down on the desk and continued perusing the website, reading more about the wines and discovering a gallery page, which included a bunch of photos of the winery, the vineyard, the Flahertys, and their customers. He clicked through them, hoping to see a picture of Kitt.

In all the pictures, people seemed to be enjoying themselves, sipping wine, listening to live music, and picnicking on the deck and the grounds around the big barn. Aidan had once told him that every day at a winery was a happy day, and the photos certainly bore that out. Even the ones of Conor and Sean trimming vines and bottling wine and messing with huge stainless-steel tanks showed joyful, laughing winemakers at work. Ah! There it was—a smiling Kitt standing by a table holding up a masterpiece by one of her valentine makers last month.

Rye grabbed his phone again and tapped the message icon. *"What the hell is a toasty nose?"* After a few seconds and a deep breath, he hit the Send arrow.

"Who is this?"

He played along, even though he suspected she probably knew it was him. *"Rye. I'm looking at the FIBW website and this white—chardonnay—says it has a toasty nose. Seriously? That sounds painful."*

He hoped she was laughing because that was what he was imagining. Kitt wearing something comfortable yet sexy, sitting on her sofa or even in her bed... *No, no, don't imagine her in bed, Lange. Big mistake when you're at work.*

"LOL. It's a way to describe the scent of a wine that has been aged in oak barrels. When you inhale the scent of the wine, you get a toasty nuance."

A toasty nuance, huh? Okay, sure. He tapped his finger against his teeth before typing, *"Like breakfast toast?"*

"Yup."

"Interesting. What are you doing?"

"Drinking a cup of tea, forcing myself to leave my notebook closed. You?"

"I'm at the station, catching up on paperwork."

"Is that how you typically spend a Friday night?"

"Yes. Pretty much."

"That's not what I've heard."

Rye chuckled. Friday nights were frequently his time to catch up on stuff he'd let slide during the week, so he could start Monday with a clean slate. Sometimes, if work was caught up, he took a pizza or pad Thai to either Max or Beck, depending on which of his brothers was working a twenty-four-hour shift. He thought for a minute, then texted, *"I'm a hard-working cop, have some respect."*

"I do. I've seen you in action, remember?" She added a

wine bottle emoji and a car with lights on top of it.

"I remember." Immediately, Kitt's walking the line in the post office parking lot popped into his head, and he almost moaned aloud.

"Why are you looking at our website? You don't drink wine."

"Curiosity, mostly. It's a long, circuitous route from what I was thinking about when I should be working to your website to toasty nose. One day I'll tell you about it."

"I'll look forward to that." A long pause. At first, he thought she'd stopped texting. Suddenly, *"Are you coming to the dance tomorrow night?"*

With his heart in his throat, he responded as honestly as he could. *"I think I lost the bet. I wasn't sure I'd be welcome."*

After a few beats, she responded. *"It's not over until midnight, copper, but I'd venture to say it was a draw."*

"I kissed you."

"I kissed you right back."

She sure had. He could still feel her lips opening to his, which brought a whole new onslaught to his senses that was making him shift uncomfortably in his squeaky office chair. He wanted nothing more than to drive over to her apartment and work on that whole kissing and kissing right back thing. They were starting to get pretty good at it. A few more times and he was certain they'd become experts.

What if he suggested he stop by? The paperwork could wait. It was quiet in the station. Duane was in his office, and a couple of the younger cops were out on the front desk. He could leave if he chose… But was it fair to go to her? She was right; the bet wasn't officially over until midnight and it was still only—he glanced at the clock above the door—ten fifteen. He hovered his thumbs over the keyboard.

"Let's call it a draw, okay? Can I see you…now?"

He waited. And waited. Minutes ticked by and it was ten twenty, then ten thirty and she still hadn't answered. *Dammit.* He shoved his chair back, the *skreek* echoing in the empty bullpen, and paced to the window. Staring out at the county corrections facility across the street, he curled his hands into fists, stretched his fingers, and fisted them again.

The crescendo of anxiety at this new dynamic in his life—this uncertainty around a woman—was alternately exasperating and exhilarating. He hated not being sure of what she was thinking but loved hoping it was about him. Before, he always knew what a woman expected from him and he provided it…until he didn't. Until he simply walked away. It was easy, he always knew exactly what to do and say to keep things going his way. Kitt, on the other hand, was an enigma. The more of a wall she put up, the more he longed to scale it and—

His phone rang and he nearly tripped over two chairs getting back to his desk. He grabbed it without even looking at the screen. Taking a deep breath, he answered in his best cop manner, "Lange."

"Ryker? I need you." It was Kitt, speaking so softly, he could barely hear her; the worry in her voice told him this call had nothing to do with the two of them or the bet.

"Kitt? What's going on?"

"Can you come over to my flat, please? I've got a…a situation here."

"I'll be right there." He ended the call, shrugged into his coat, and headed out. At the door, he hesitated for a second, went back to his desk, unlocked it, retrieved his service revolver from the middle drawer, and clipped it into his inside-the-waistband holster. She didn't sound frightened, merely apprehensive, but it never hurt to be prepared.

Chapter Sixteen

KITT HAD NEVER been so happy to see anyone in her life as she was to see Lieutenant Ryker Lange standing on the landing outside her apartment above Mac Mackenzie's garage. "It's open," she called at his brisk knock. She would've gotten up to answer the door, except she had her hands full. She could only imagine what was going through Ryker's head when he opened the door and took in the scene before him.

Josh Davis sat on the table in front of the sofa, his knees bumping Kitt's, as he held his left arm close to his body. His twin brother, Caleb, cuddled next to Kitt on the couch, holding a bag of frozen peas to his right eye. She was busy wiping his face with a rag that had quite a bit of blood on it. Both boys' faces were tear-stained and Josh's knees trembled against Kitt's when he saw his "big brother" open the door.

Rye shut the door and rushed forward. "What the... Josh? Caleb? What happened? What are you guys doing *here*?"

Josh's voice trembled. "We didn't know where else to go. You weren't home. Caleb remembered that when we went

191

fishing, somebody said Kitt lived over Mr. Mackenzie's garage, so we came here. I had to get Caleb inside—he was bleeding and he didn't have his jacket."

Rye met Kitt's eyes over Josh's head before kneeling down beside the boy. "Josh, tell me what happened."

"*He* smacked Caleb…twice…and…and when I tried to stop him from doing it again, he grabbed my arm…hard. It hurts, Rye." Eyes sparking with anger and shimmering with tears, Josh started to move his arm, then winced and kept it tucked next to his skinny chest.

Rye touched his thin shoulder and Kitt tilted her head toward Josh. "I think it might be dislocated. They wouldn't let me call 9-9-9…no, wait, I mean, 9-1-1. Insisted I find you instead."

Rye stood and came around the table. When he lifted the bag of peas from Caleb's face, he sucked in a breath. "God almighty."

Kitt noticed how gently he stroked the boy's hair off his forehead as he set the package back on Caleb's eye, which seemed to be getting more swollen and purple with each passing moment. The cut on his cheek had finally stopped bleeding, thank heaven, as had his nose. She pulled her arm out from around the boy and rose, hitching her chin to indicate she wanted Rye to follow her to the kitchen.

"That bastard!" Rye hissed, his gray eyes nearly black in the dim light of the kitchen. "I'm going to beat the living crap out of him."

Kitt didn't blame him for being angry; she was furious herself. However, they had to figure out what to do—both boys needed a hospital, but they'd begged her not to take them over to St. Mark's before Ryker got there. "I know, I know. And I'll give ye a hand at thrashin' him when that time comes." She soothed Rye with a hand on his forearm. "Our first concern, though, is gettin' these lads some help. Where's their mother?"

Rye leaned over the counter. "Josh, where's your mom?"

Josh gave a grim laugh. "Passed out. *He* brought home a new bottle of tequila. They were doing shots at the table while we watched TV." Josh grimaced in pain. "He came after us because we couldn't find the remote fast enough to turn down the sound."

Without moving, Caleb added, "It was my fault. I didn't know I was sitting on it."

Kitt swallowed hard, appalled that a twelve-year-old kid would refer so casually to doing shots, let alone be aware that his mother was passed out, and not just sleeping. Josh and Caleb had seen way too much in their young lives. She hadn't even realized she was gripping Ryker's arm until he put his hand over hers.

Tears burned her eyelids. "Oh, Ryker, I hate this! Those boys shouldn't ever see their mom like that."

Rye shook his head. "Yeah, well, you grow up fast at River Run." He squeezed her hand before heading back out to the living room with her hot on his heels. "Guys, we gotta get you to a doc. I'm gonna text my brother Max and see if he's working the ER tonight."

Josh leaped up, wincing again as he jostled his arm. "No! If we go to the ER, they'll have to call *him*, and he'll come and get us and he'll be so mad. He's gonna kill us anyway when he figures out we sneaked out while he was the bathroom. He's probably out looking for us right now."

Rye put a careful hand on Josh's hair before thumbing a text on his phone. "I'm not going to let him near you, Josh. I promise."

Caleb spoke up from the sofa, sounding dejected and remarkably adult. "Joshie, we gotta get your arm fixed and I think the cut above my eye needs stitches. Jed's damn ring cut me pretty bad." He took the peas away from his face so Kitt could take a look, his expression abashed. "Sorry, Kitt, I meant his *darn* ring."

Sure enough, there was deep cut buried in the swollen, bruised flesh below his brow. "Oh, darlin', nobody blames ye for cursin' at a time like this." She pressed a kiss to the top of his head. "Ryker, let's get them to the hospital. We can figure it out from there."

Ryker's phone chimed. "Okay, Max is on duty. He's waiting for us."

A lump grew in Kitt's throat when Ryker took off his puffy winter jacket and helped Caleb into it before herding the two of them out of the apartment and down the stairs. She grabbed her own coat and also an extra plaid winter scarf off the hooks by the front door. When they got down to the truck, she wrapped it around Rye's neck before hopping into the backseat with Caleb.

Rye tossed her a quick smile as he eased Josh into the front passenger seat and ran around to jump in and start the truck. He reached across Josh to get the seat belt, then at the boy's instinctive cry of protest, patted his knee instead. "Okay, no belt, but sit tight and hold on with your other hand, okay?"

"Just drive," Josh replied through gritted teeth.

Rye backed out of the drive and was on Main Street in less than a minute, driving fast but carefully, clearly watching out for Josh's shoulder.

Caleb pulled on Kitt's sleeve. "Kitt, my nose is bleeding again. I don't want to get blood on Rye's jacket."

"Don't worry about that jacket, buddy, it washes." Rye opened the console between him and Josh, yanked out a fistful of fast-food napkins, and tossed them over his shoulder.

Kitt caught them as they floated into her lap and handed a couple to Caleb. "Here, poppet, hold this to your nose." She guided his hand. "Now tip your head back."

"Owww." Caleb's eyes filled with tears. "Do you think my nose is broken?"

"Gently now." Kitt stroked his hair back and turned over the now-mushy-but-still-cold bag of peas on his eye. "I don't think it's broken—it's not too swollen and it's still straight."

Ryker caught her eye in the rearview mirror and his expression made her stomach flip. She wouldn't have been surprised to see steam coming out of his ears, he was so angry, yet his face only showed gratitude, so she gave him an encouraging smile as he pulled into the St. Mark's parking lot and under the canopy at the Emergency entrance.

Max, looking burly and professional all at the same time in his navy-blue scrubs, shot out the door with two other people clad in navy scrubs and opened the passenger side of the truck. "What've we got here?"

"I think his shoulder's dislocated." Rye kept a hand on Josh's back as Max helped the kid out of the truck and into a wheelchair.

"Take him to exam two and help him get his shirt off. And call CPS." Max shoved the seatback forward. "And what's this guy's sto—" He furrowed his brow, then grinned. "Hey there, Kitt. How ya doin'? Who've you got here?"

Kitt smiled. "This is Caleb, he got hit in the face. The worst is his eye I think, but his nose has been bleeding and his cheek is cut. Poppet, you know Dr. Max, don't you?"

Caleb waved feebly. "Yeah, he's the doc on standby at the basketball games." When he raised his head, the bag of peas fell off his eye and a thin stream of blood ran down to his lip again. Kitt managed not to wince at the eye, which was a mess, and simply handed him more napkins before sliding out to stand on the pavement so Max could lift Caleb gently out of the truck.

Rye got out and came around to help Max. "Any way you can put them in the same exam room? They need to be together tonight," he asked in a hushed tone.

Kitt caught the touching request as she stepped back to give them room, and her heart opened up as she watched him hover over Caleb, concern and love etched on his handsome face. She touched Ryker's shoulder. "Why don't you go with the boys? I'll park your truck and come meet you. That is, if you trust me to drive it."

Rye nodded and followed her around to the driver's side,

holding the door for her to slip in under the wheel. Before he shut the door, he leaned in and touched his lips to her cheek. "Thanks," he whispered, then grinned and winked. "Oh, hey, Irish. Keep right."

THE WAITING AREA was empty except for Rye, who'd come out to wait for the boys' aunt and uncle, who were on their way from Rising Sun a few miles east up the river. Kitt was back in the exam room with the boys. They were both doing better, thanks to Max and the great staff at St. Mark's. He'd been grateful for how accommodating and kind the nurses had been, bringing an extra bed into the largest exam room so the kids could be together, teasing and joking with them to ease their fears.

As he paced in front of the tall windows that overlooked the parking lot, Rye tried to corral his jumbled thoughts. He'd never been so impressed with his little brother, who handled both boys with professionalism and tender concern. Max had given Josh a mild sedative and while they waited for that to take effect, he called an ophthalmologist in to check Caleb's eye, as well as a plastic surgeon friend of his to stitch up the cut below the boy's brow and the one on his cheek. When Josh's pain meds kicked in, he'd let Rye stand by and distract Josh while he performed what he called a "closed reduction," which basically turned out to be Max manipulating the kid's shoulder until it popped back into place.

Rye had to hand it to young Josh—he hadn't made a

sound throughout the whole thing. But when Max declared the process a success and told the nurse to find him a sling, Josh's eyes filled with tears and Rye's heart ached. He'd sat down on the bed and taken him in his arms, letting the kid cry his heart out against his chest. Kitt had stuck close to Caleb, holding his hand while the nurse cleaned up his face for the surgeon and put a new ice pack on his eye.

There was a moment of panic when the registration clerk came in to take care of the paperwork and he realized that neither he nor Kitt had any authority to sign for the boys' treatment. Then he remembered that in his glove box, he had a consent-to-treat form that Lori had given him when she signed the boys up for the Big Brothers program. He rushed down to his truck to grab it and the copy of Lori's insurance card that she'd stapled to it. He handed it all to the registrar with a triumphant grin before scrolling in his phone for Lori's sister's number. He'd used it before, more than once, when Lori had been too drunk for him to leave the boys at home with her.

He and Max had consulted with the CPS social worker on call and, over Josh's and Caleb's objections, had her photograph the twins' injuries when they first arrived. Rye assured them it was standard procedure in child abuse cases and what Jed had done certainly constituted child abuse. Rye phoned Duane Wilson to send an officer to take the boys' statements while Kitt had gone back and forth between their beds with calm reassurances and words of comfort.

"They're both sleepin'." Kitt's voice spun him around. She looked spent, in spite of the faint smile on her face.

He went to her. "How can I ever thank you for tonight?" He searched her lovely face, longing to pull her into his arms and kiss her, but this was neither the time nor the place. Instead, he took both her hands in his. "Those boys are crazy about you, you know that?"

"Aye." She closed her eyes for a second. "And I'm crazy about them as well, poor wee lambs. What will happen to them?"

He tightened his fingers around hers. "Their aunt Liz sounded mighty determined when I spoke to her. She and her husband should be here any minute. I think Child Protective Services will let them take the twins until something can be worked out. We've been down this road before. This isn't the first time she's had to step in…just the worst."

Kitt shook her head sadly. "How I hate the cruelty in the world. What kind of monster hurts a child like that? And how does their mother allow it?"

Rye stopped resisting and pulled her into his arms, inhaling the citrus-sweet scent of her hair. "She's an alcoholic and Jed's an enabler. The boys are caught in the middle of a toxic relationship. I'm glad Liz and Tom are coming for them. They love those kids and it's entirely mutual. Maybe this time they'll get to keep them…at least until Lori gets some help and divorces that bastard."

When she wrapped her arms around his waist and laid her head against his shoulder, her whole body sagged, and he realized how truly exhausted she must be. "As soon as Liz and Tom get here, I'm taking you home, okay?"

She merely nodded against his sweater. "The lads were

blamin' themselves for what happened. Thinkin' if they hadn't had the sound turned up or if Caleb hadn't sat on the bloody remote or Josh hadn't told that rat to leave Caleb alone… Dear Lord, it breaks my heart."

He lifted her chin to look into her face. "What was that song you were singing to Caleb back there?"

"Just an old lullaby Móraí—my grandmother—used to sing it to us when we were wee ones."

"Sing it to me."

"Here?"

He glanced around the dim waiting area, lit only by a couple of lamps and the snack machine in the corner. "Nobody here but you and me. Why not?"

She smiled shyly, closed her eyes, and slowly began a murmuring tune about the moon and the stars and larks and mountains that turned into words he didn't recognize at all. Her voice was a sweet contralto that fit the old tune perfectly. When she finished, her cheeks were rosy with embarrassment.

He grinned. "That's beautiful. Was that Gaelic at the end?"

"Aye. We don't really speak it that much at home. Móraí did…always." The lilt in her voice sent a shiver through him.

He pressed a kiss to her forehead. "I'll tell you somethin', lass, your brogue is about the sexiest thing I've ever heard." He gave it his best Irish reading, delighted when she giggled.

"You've a gift for imitation, Lieutenant, as well as gift for blather."

"My degree was in secondary ed, but I minored in

French and German. I really enjoy languages," he confessed.

She leaned back in his arms to gaze up at him, her eyes full of curiosity. "How'd you end up a copper? That's an odd twist."

He shrugged. "I wanted to come back to teach at River's Edge, but they weren't hiring when I graduated. The police department was, though, and Duane talked me into going to the academy."

"Are ye ever sorry? I mean, that you're not a teacher?"

"Nope." He shook his head firmly. "Police work is interesting, I still get to work with kids, and I'm serving the town I love."

Kitt gazed up at him, her head cocked. "You're a good man, Lieutenant Lange."

Left-tenant made him weak in the knees and, for a nanosecond, it was a coin toss who was holding up whom. For the second time in as many days, someone told him he was a *good man* and his heart expanded at the idea of being known that way. As he and Kitt stood in the middle of the hospital reception area, holding on to each other like two drowning sailors, it was as though the world had paused, neither of them quite knowing what might follow.

Chapter Seventeen

WARMTH AND THE scent of bacon frying hit Rye as he opened the door to the Riverside Diner early the next morning. Mac waved to him from behind the counter. "Coffee's hot and fresh."

"Thank the Lord." Rye scooted onto a stool. "It was a long night. I need coffee and pancakes."

"Carly, pour some more batter on the griddle, babe; we've got a hungry policeman here." Mac filled a mug and set it and a pitcher of half-and-half in front of Rye. "Um, understand you had yourself quite an interesting evening, Lieutenant."

Rye glanced over his shoulder at the table where Noah, Clyde, Harry Evans, who was now a circuit court judge, and Butch Carter, the owner of the double H, sat. The Breakfast Club, as the four older gentlemen had come to be known, opened Mac's nearly every morning. "What have you heard?"

"That you arrested Jed Cochran and he's cooling his heels in the county lockup."

"That I did and he is." Rye dribbled half-and-half into his coffee.

"And you and Kitt took the twins to the ER?"

Rye nodded. "Yup."

"We saw you fly by as we were getting home from Conor and Sam's last night." Mac said, still holding the coffeepot as he eyed his customers.

"The boys were hurt."

Mac reached behind him and got a napkin-wrapped set of silverware to place before Rye. "Kitt told us about it this morning when she stopped for coffee. Sounds like it was a hot mess."

Rye took a sip of steaming coffee. "It was. Liz and Tom came over to get the boys from the hospital. Tom took them over to Rising Sun, and Liz rode with Duane and me to make the arrest. Waited outside until we had Jed in custody, then went in to stay with Lori. Liz was going to try to convince her to check herself into Turning Point in Louisville."

Mac offered a faint smile. "She came by earlier to grab a couple of coffees, driving Lori's car and had Lori in the front seat. Maybe they were headed there."

"God, I hope so. Liz and Tom will take good care of the twins, but we'll probably need restraining orders to keep Jed away from the boys and Lori."

"I can do that." Harry Evans spoke up from the table behind Rye. "We all heard what happened." He jerked a thumb toward Noah. "Dot's cousin Pauline was working registration at St. Mark's when you and Kitt brought the boys in. How are they doing?"

Carly set a steaming plate on the service pass-through.

"Pickup table five."

Norma, the breakfast server, sauntered behind the counter to tray up four plates and take them to a tableful of early risers, while Mac took a pot of fresh-brewed coffee out to offer warm-ups to anyone who needed it.

Rye swung around on his stool to face the Saturday morning breakfast crowd that consisted mostly of shop owners and their employees. "Be best if we didn't make this the hot topic of the day, folks. It's an ongoing investigation and also, Lori and the kids need our support, not to be gossiped about over bacon and eggs. Okay?"

Noah Barker nodded firmly and Butch gave a thumbs-up as a murmur of agreement rolled through the diner and everyone went back to their food.

Clyde Schwimmer cleared his throat loudly as Rye started to turn back to the counter. "Hey, Rye. On another subject, it's Valentine's Day. Who won the bet?"

"Yeah, you going stag to the dance tonight?" Harry chimed in.

Rye spun his stool around slowly and gave that table of gents a hard stare over the top of his glasses. "Any chance we could leave that topic alone, too?"

Noah grinned. "No chance in a hell."

Rye sighed when the others hooted and laughed. "Well, I don't know the answer to that yet, so you bunch of cackling old hens are going to have to wait until tonight. Doesn't matter anyway since that stash of cash Hugh is holding for you at the pub is going straight into the collection plate tomorrow morning." He cast his glance over the whole room. "Am I right?"

The laughter changed to grumbling, so Rye turned back to the counter, where Norma was setting down a plate of steaming pancakes slathered in butter. "You know one of the best parts about eating breakfast here every morning, Norma?"

Norma gave him a wink as she placed a pitcher of syrup next to him. "I know, I know. My smiling face."

"Actually, I was going to say locally sourced maple syrup and butter, but your face is very nice, too." Rye dug into the pancakes, closing his eyes at the first delicious bite. "Mmmm…"

"What? No come-ons this morning? No begging for a kiss?" Norma's brow rose almost into her wispy bangs. "Where's my usual morning invitation to join you in your warm squad car for a quick round of slap-and-tickle, Lieutenant? You weren't required to stop flirting with *every* woman, only Kitt." She frowned as she gazed at him for a moment. "And hey, what's with the professor look? I mean, it totally works for you, but what happened to your contacts?"

Rye took another bite of pancakes, chewing slowly and thoughtfully before he rested his fork on the edge of his plate and picked up his coffee. He hesitated, swallowing the automatic playful response that rose to his lips. Instead, he leaned his elbow on the table, resting his chin in his palm. "Tell me about your photographs, Norma." He pointed to the newest clipping on Mac's town news bulletin board. "I've seen you out and about with your camera, but I had no idea you took such amazing pictures until I saw the one you entered in the newspaper photo contest—the one of your grandson watching the *River Queen* at sunrise…wow. You deserved that first-place award! That picture is really beautiful." He took a sip of coffee, waiting for her to pick her jaw up off the counter.

"Th-thank you, Rye." Norma's normally coquettish expression toned down to genuine quiet smile. "That's so nice of you to say."

"How'd you get it all to come together so perfectly? I mean, the sunrise, the boat, Christopher laughing—you have a great eye." It was a new tack—not automatically going for the flirtatious back-and-forth with every woman he met, merely complimenting a friend. It felt damn good. *Right.*

As she haltingly began to talk about the picture, it shocked the heck out of him that he was sincerely interested. His eyes had been opened by his attraction to Kitt. That longing to know everything about *her* had somehow suddenly extended to women he'd been around all his life but never bothered to truly know. Women like Norma. He glanced around the diner when she slipped away to deliver another tray of food.

There was Janet, sitting in the corner booth showing Alice Dawson her latest knitting project, and Lianne Morrison, the therapist at St. Mark's, sipping coffee with Sandy from the flower shop and her daughter, Joannie, who was the drama coach at the high school. His heart warmed at the sight Gia Bishop, Sam's paralegal, and Britney, the gym teacher at the elementary school, laughing together over plates of Carly's crème brûlée French toast. So many smart and talented women in his life and up until now, he'd missed knowing all their complex layers because he'd never bothered to go beyond playful banter.

Suddenly, the urge to see Kitt overwhelmed him. He needed to talk to her. She had to know him, to know his fear of becoming his father and how that had affected every relationship he'd ever had. He wanted to tell her about his talk with Harley. He wanted to ask her to talk to him about what had happened in Ireland. He wanted to beg her to allow him help her get past the fear of being hurt and let him into her heart.

Digging his wallet out of his pocket, he tucked a ten under his plate for Norma, swiped his Visa at the register, and with a smile, accepted the cardboard to-go cup that Mac held out to him. As he headed for the door, his gaze fixed on a nearby booth where Conor, Sean, and Brendan Flaherty sat scarfing down waffles and bacon and talking earnestly. Almost as if he sensed Rye's presence, Bren turned his head, then raised his hand and beckoned Rye to their table.

From the looks on their faces, they had something serious to discuss and, you might know, the one time he needed an ally, his buddy Aidan was nowhere to be seen. He sucked in a deep breath and ambled over to the table. "Hey, guys."

Bren scooted over. "Have a seat, man."

Rye perched on the edge of the booth seat. "What's up?"

They all appeared so solemn, he worried that they were going to tell him someone had died. Finally, Sean spoke up. "Look, Rye, we're all friends here, so we're just going to say this flat out."

Rye's fingers clenched around the cardboard cup of coffee so hard that he feared the lid would pop off, so he set it on the table in front of him. "What do you want to say?"

Conor leaned forward, barely missing dragging his sleeve through the syrup on his plate. "Here's the thing. Don't mess with Kitt, okay? That jackwad in Ireland really did a number on her. She's vulnerable and she's dope sick for you, man."

Rye wiped his sweaty palms on his jeans and forced himself not to grin like an idiot at the news that Kitt was falling for him. "I'm not *messing* with her." He rubbed his chin and sighed before meeting Sean's blue gaze, so like Kitt's. "I'm in love with her. Have been from the first moment I saw her." He shook his head when they all three stared at him in bewilderment. "You oughta know that feeling, Con. Haven't you always said that you fell in love with Sam the moment you saw her?"

Conor chuckled. "I did. She was dripping wet and cussing at a flat tire."

Rye eyed Bren. "And you? How soon after you got back in town did you lose your heart to Tierney?"

Brendan's grin was as infectious as Kitt's. "I took longer—I had to separate Tee, the skinny kid in pigtails, from Tierney, the gorgeous woman she'd become." He shrugged. "We did everything bass-ackward, but I knew I was a goner the first time I kissed her."

Rye raised one brow at Sean. "And Meg?"

Sean's scowl turned into a smile. "Aw hell, I'd known her

practically all my life, but I fell in love when she was the first thing I saw after I'd been shot. She drove to Chicago and was right there for me. She always had been. That's when I knew she was the one."

Rye shrugged. "Then you all get it, yeah?" He gazed from face to face to face for few seconds. "If this is you guys thinking you might have to go all *Hitmen* on my ass, you can stand down. I promise, if I can win her, I'll love her with all my heart."

Brendan fell into a brogue that was as spot-on as if he'd just stepped off the boat from Ireland himself. "Damn, who'd have thought a mere slip of a lass from County Wexford would bring down River's Edge's favorite cad and scallywag? So ye love her, aye? What are you plannin' to do about it, boyo?"

Rye stood up, and with a tinge of pride, imitated Bren's Irish accent perfectly. "I'm not sure about anythin' at all these days. Me 'ead and me 'eart are all over the place. I *do* know this, lads"—he picked up his coffee—"everythin' makes perfect sense whenever I'm with her, and that's never happened before Kitt."

Bren's chuckle turned into a full-on laugh. "Lord, man, please tell me you'll audition for Aidan and the *Queen* this spring. You need to be onstage crooning 'Danny Boy.'"

"Ah, if only I could sing." Grinning, he walked out to a rousing round of applause from the Flahertys, the kitchen staff, and the Breakfast Club.

"MAEVE, COME ON. Help me pick one. I'm runnin' out of time here." Kitt couldn't believe she was *still* standing in her underwear in a dressing room at Cinderella's Closet, the women's clothing boutique Holly had recommended. The shop took up both floors in an old Victorian house on the corner of Broadway and Fifth and had a vast selection of new, consigned, and vintage clothing. The second floor was all dresses and so far, Kitt had tried on at least eight that she thought might work for the dance, which was a mere—she glanced at her watch—five hours away.

Yanking on another dress, she twisted in front of the three-way mirror, her back to the phone that she'd propped up on a gilt chair. "This one will work, won't it?" In the mirror, she caught Maeve wrinkling her nose onscreen. "*What?* What's wrong with it?"

"There's a giant bow stuck to your arse." Maeve's voice was loud but tinny from nearly six thousand kilometers away. "No way. Not that one."

"But it's red." Kitt released a frustrated breath and reached for the zip on the side of the dress. "I want a red dress tonight. It's Valentine's Day. It has to be—"

Maeve giggled. "Killer? Something that will drop that copper to his knees?"

Kitt glanced over her shoulder at her phone. Why bother denying it? Her sister knew her better than anyone else in the world. "Aye. Right to his bloody knees."

"Try the hot pink one again. It's—" A knock on the fitting room door interrupted Maeve's suggestion.

Kitt cracked the door and peered around it. "Yes?"

"Here, miss." The older woman who'd been helping her stood there with a large box. "Here's something else for you to try. It's a vintage cocktail dress from the 1920s. I think it would be perfect on your tall, slim frame. And I've got a lovely black knitted shawl that will go with it just fine."

Kitt pulled back the door and held her breath as she watched the woman open the box and draw the tissue paper from around the red-and-black beaded chemise-style dress. When she held it up, Kitt gulped. *This is it.* The dress of her dreams. She squirmed impatiently as the clerk helped her slip it over her head. There were no zippers or buttons; it was simply a two-layer silky gown that hung straight from her shoulders to her knees. The red under-dress showed through a black lacy over-layer that shimmered with crystal beads. She turned this way and that in front of the mirror, trying to see the gorgeous dress from every angle, loving how the fabric seemed to move with her.

On the phone, Maeve gasped in obvious delight. "Oh, Kitten! That's the one! You look fabulous!"

The woman chuckled softly. "I knew it would be you." She gazed at Kitt for a long moment and Kitt noticed she appeared to have tears in her eyes.

"What is it?" she asked, placing one hand on the woman's arm. "Are ye okay?"

"I'm fine." The older woman swiped at her eyes under her glasses. "It's a Lanvin original from Paris. It was my grandmother's. She was a French war bride after World War I and came to America with my grandfather in the twenties. She was the daughter of a very wealthy Parisian businessman, who wasn't thrilled she was moving to America, but move she did with a brand-new husband and fifteen trunks of clothes and linens all loaded onto the *SS Paris*.

"I have a picture of her when she wore this dress to a Valentine's Day party in Louisville in 1927." Kitt's heart went out to her as a faraway smile crossed the clerk's lips before she shook her head briskly. "Anyway, when I started this shop almost fifteen years ago, it was mainly a consignment store. My mother brought me all of Gran's designer clothes that she'd kept over the years. They were too nice to give to charity and yet, neither she nor I would ever fit into them." She glanced ruefully at her well-padded body. "Besides, where would we wear them? But I couldn't bear to put them out on the racks for sale, so I donated a few to Newfield's, the art museum in Indy. The rest I kept boxed in acid-free tissue, waiting for the right person to come along. Over the years, I've had customers come in that I was certain one of Gran's gowns would be perfect for. I only have two left. This is one of them."

"It's exquisite," Kitt breathed.

The woman stepped up and draped a lightweight knitted shawl over Kitt's bare upper arms. "Here you go. This will keep you warm, although if you're going to the dance at the winery, I doubt staying warm will be a problem."

Kitt stared at her reflection stunned at how incredible she looked. "I'm so beautiful!" she burst out and then her cheeks heated at her own audacity. "I-I mean…"

The salesclerk smiled. "You *are* lovely."

Kitt was almost afraid to ask the obvious question. "How

much is it?"

"You'll want to pin your hair up, but leave a few wispy tendrils." The clerk demonstrated, holding Kitt's long hair up off her shoulders. "In 1923, Gran paid around one hundred and thirty dollars for that dress, which was more than the clothing budget for a *whole year* for a regular working girl way back then. It's yours for that price and the shawl is my gift to you because you remind me so much of Gran."

Kitt's heart pounded. "I-I can't take this gown and the shawl for so little. It's no—"

Maeve's voice from the phone interrupted her. "Of course you can, Kitt. Don't you see you're bringin' joy to Ms.—I'm sorry, we don't know your name."

The woman glanced down at the phone. "I'm Pam Keys."

Maeve waved from the screen. "To Ms. Keys here, who has such fond memories of her gran?"

Pam scooped up the other dresses. "She's absolutely right. Now, get dressed and fold the gown back into the box. It's not fragile. However, you don't ever want to hang it. Always store it flat in the box. I'll meet you out front."

After one more long look in the mirror, Kitt gently tugged the gown over her head, folded it carefully, and rewrapped it in the tissue, exactly as it had been when Pam opened the box. While Kitt put her jeans and sweatshirt back on, Maeve chattered eagerly, making her promise to have one of the cousins take pictures so she could share them with the rest of the family there in Ireland.

At the checkout, she handed over her Visa, talking shoes with Pam as she rang up the purchase. Kitt couldn't decide between her sexy, though incredibly uncomfortable black stilettos or her black kitten heels with the rhinestone buckles.

"Go for comfort. The kitten heels will be more authentic and work better since you'll be dancing—at least I hope you'll be dancing." She turned the point-of-sale screen. "Sign here." She waited as Kitt signed with her finger. "You enjoy, honey. Some guy is going to be dazzled when he sees you tonight."

Kitt wet her lips, her heart soaring at the thought of Ryker's face when he got a look at her in this remarkable dress. "Aye, wouldn't that be lovely? I've never dazzled anyone before."

Pam wrapped the shawl in tissue and tucked it into a bag with the box. "I find that hard to believe, a beautiful girl like you."

Heat filled Kitt's cheeks and impulsively she zipped around the counter and hugged the woman. "Thank you feels inadequate, Pam."

Pam returned the hug. "All I ask is that I get a full report with pictures."

"I promise!" Kitt practically skipped out the door, already imagining Ryker's reaction when he got a look at her in the vintage gown. *You're the one.* His words replayed in her head for the hundredth time.

So are you, Lieutenant Lange, so are you.

Chapter Eighteen

THE GRAND ENTRANCE Kitt had hoped to make at the Valentine Dance didn't come off quite as she'd planned. First of all, the hustle of getting the rest of the decorations finished and arranging a dance floor among the high-top tables took way longer than she'd expected. Not that she didn't have lots of help. Carly and Mac, along with Harley Cole, who'd arrived early to lend a hand, set up the hors d'oeuvres table. The variety of delectable goodies made Kitt's stomach growl and she nabbed a tiny quiche from the steamy pan behind the table, earning a fake hand slap and a wink from Mac.

"Paula's heart-shaped frosted cookies are the perfect dessert tonight!" she exclaimed, nabbing one of those, as well, when she realized it had been hours since she'd had lunch. "Just *one* of those yummy-looking bacon things, too, Mac, please? I'm starvin'."

Mac held the pan out to her, while Carly arranged them attractively on a doily-covered glass plate. "Oh, what the heck, help yourself. You've sure earned it. This place looks great."

Aidan had finished hanging the last of the long pink and red crepe paper streamers when Holly arrived, breathless, carrying huge trash bags filled with the wired cotton clouds that she and her mom, Melinda, had spent several weeks creating.

"I'm so sorry I'm late, Kitt!" Holly panted as she pulled off her jacket. "The heat in the café went out and I had to wait on the guy to come fix it."

"No worries. These are perfect, Holly!" Kitt got busy pulling giant airy puffs from the bags and handing them to Aidan to hang around the shiny silver disco ball with clear fishing line. "Is it fixed?"

Holly nodded. "Finally! I practically had to promise him my right arm and a pint of blood."

Aidan sighed from his perch on the ladder. "Honey, please let me replace that old furnace, okay? This is the third time since November you've had to call the repairman."

Kitt had to smile as Holly shook her head vehemently. "It's good now. Besides you have to reroof the *Queen* this spring and a new furnace would cost a fortune."

Aidan looked down at her, affection clear on his handsome face. "Once again, we *have* a fortune, so we can—" He closed his lips at the warning in Holly's expression. "Okay. Okay. I'm not saying anything more."

Holly gave him a dazzling smile. "Thank you, my love."

Sean, Bren, and Conor opened wine bottles behind the tasting bar, while Sam and Meg organized racks of gleaming glasses. Kitt looked at her watch for the thousandth time. The DJ was late, Bren needed to get back to get Tierney, who was trying to get dressed and keep Maggie happy at the same time as she waited for her parents, Teresa and Frank, to arrive. The Ashtons, along with Holly and Aidan's son, Mateo, were on babysitting detail, rounding up all the Flaherty children and watching them at Conor and Sam's house during the dance.

Kitt still had to get dressed, too. She'd brought her clothes and makeup to the ridge to avoid having to return to her apartment in town before the dance. She shivered in anticipation at the thought of the vintage frock waiting for her in Conor and Sam's guest room.

Clapping her hands to get everyone's attention, she called, "Okay, everybody! Listen! This place looks amazing! The decorations are perfect! The electric candles are so romantic and the dimmed lights and the fireplace...wow." A lump grew in her throat as she saw how they'd managed to turn the huge high-ceilinged room into a dreamy, intimate venue. "Thank you all so much! If folks don't feel the love tonight, they're hopeless."

Conor grinned. "Speaking of hopeless and in love, I see our favorite police lieutenant down in the parking lot helping the DJ unload."

Kitt flew to the window. Ryker was indeed standing at the back of Mobile Music's SUV as the DJ loaded equipment into his arms. "Oh, no! I don't want him to see me like *this*!"

Sean smirked. "Why does it matter? It's not like he's your date, *is he*?"

Kitt narrowed her eyes and held out her hand. "Your

keys, please, you wanker. My car's out front, so I've got to sneak out the back."

"C'mon. My car's out back, too. I'll drive you down to Con's," Harley volunteered, giving a fan of hot pink napkins a final tap on the buffet table.

"KITT, YOU LOOK"—HARLEY'S jaw dropped as Kitt came out of the bathroom in her new-old dress and did a runway turn—"simply fantastic!"

In the mirror above the dresser, Kitt could see her cheeks turning rosy. "Thanks, Harley. And thanks so much for doing my hair! I look like I'm all ready for a party at Gertrude Stein's in 1925 Paris. All I need is F. Scott Fitzgerald or Ernest Hemingway to be my date."

Harley eyed her, one brow quirked. "I'm pretty sure you have a date right here in the twenty-first century."

Kitt met her gaze in the mirror and nodded slowly as a frisson of pleasure sparked through her. "I think maybe I do." She rolled her lips between her teeth and bit down. "I guess I'm hopelessly drawn to bad boys, aye?"

Harley rose from her perch on the side of the bed and came to stand behind Kitt, fussing with the messy chignon she'd created low on the nape of Kitt's neck, pulling a tendril out to curl enticingly over her ear. "Rye and I dated about ten years ago. I was nuts about him. When he broke up with me, I believed my heart would never heal. Of course, it did." She smiled. "Earlier this week, well...he stopped me at

Paula's to tell me how sorry he was that he'd hurt me all those years ago. His part of the bet, Kitt. Amends." She peered around Kitt's head. "He didn't have to do it. He hadn't lost the bet. He did it for me and for himself...and for you, even though I don't think he realizes it. You're getting a good man."

Kitt blinked back the tears burning behind her lids. "I know. I'm learning his heart, but thank you for telling me that, Harley." Impulsively, she hugged her new friend. Then she grabbed the small beaded cross-body bag Sam had lent her, verified that the surprise she had for Ryker was still tucked inside, and slipped her lipstick in next to it. "I guess it's time for me to face the future, aye?" Anticipation bubbled up inside her and she grinned at Harley. "Shall we go?"

RYKER HUNG HIS winter coat on the back of a tall chair and made his way to the tasting bar, searching, his gaze skimming the folks who'd already arrived. He didn't see Kitt. He did see several other early arrivals—all the Flahertys except Bren and Tierney. There was the whole Walker crew, Cameron, Joey, Jack, and Eli, who all cleaned up pretty well, he had to admit. Holly's mom, Melinda, was already on the dance floor, laughing and flirting, with Chaz LaGrotte. *Interesting.* He waved at Mac and Carly, wondering if his own mom had arrived yet. She'd turned down the ride he'd offered, saying she would meet him at the winery. He didn't see her, though.

Conor tossed him a warm smile as he approached the bar. "Rye! What can I get you? I've got some soda down here and there are bottles of water in the coolers by the buffet."

Rye hesitated before asking, "What's the best wine for a beginner?"

Conor's brows rose. "Really?"

"Yeah." Rye nodded. "If I'm going to be a part of Kitt's life, I think I'd like to learn how to drink wine like a gentleman."

"She would never ask you to do that." Conor's eyes narrowed. "Does *she* know you're going to be a part of her life?"

Rye merely smiled. "Not yet, but I've got plans. And I know she'd never expect me to drink wine just because *she* enjoys it. I've been perusing your website, though, and I'm curious." He hitched his chin toward the bottles on the counter behind the bar. "First, can I sniff the chardonnay? I want to know what a *toasty nose* smells like."

With a bemused smile, Conor opened a bottle he drew out of the fridge under the counter and poured a tiny bit in a glass. "Here, sniff."

Rye inhaled the scent of fruit, vanilla, minerals, and…he sniffed a second time. "By God, I smell toast."

"There you go. Taste it."

Rye sipped, frowned, and immediately set the glass back on the bar. "Um…not so much. I think I'll take my toast in the form of bread. Maybe you'd better pour me something you'd pour your granny. I'll start there."

"Okay." Chuckling, Conor reached under the counter and pulled out a chilled bottle of white wine. "This is our sparkling traminette—cool, crisp, not too sweet, and little bubbly."

"Sounds like a celebration wine." Rye watched the wine fizz in his glass as Conor poured.

"What are we celebrating, Lieutenant?" Kitt's voice at his back spun him around. "Pour me one, too. Aye, coz?"

Left-tenant.

In a reaction that shocked even him, Rye's knees wobbled and he had to grasp the edge of the bar to steady himself at the sight of her. She was breathtaking in a slim red-and-black beaded dress that made him think of films he'd seen about flappers and the roaring twenties and speakeasies. His fingers curled tightly into his palms and he worried that she could hear the acceleration of his heartbeat in the couple feet of distance between them. It was certainly loud in his own ears. Golden highlights in her dark hair glistened in the firelight behind her and the ghost of smile hovered on her lips. He had never seen such a smile, such a face...such absolute perfection. He couldn't even find his voice. All he could do was stare.

At last she said, "Good evening, Ryker. You're drinking wine?"

He raised his hands in supplication and his voice was croaky when it finally came back to him. "I-I thought I'd give it a try."

"You picked a nice one." She took her glass from Conor and tilted it toward Rye's. "What shall we drink to?"

Hand trembling, Rye reached for his glass. "You." He cursed his sudden inability to produce a complete sentence in the presence of a beautiful woman. "I-I mean… no… yeah. Yes. To you." He clinked glasses with her and hoping to ease his dry mouth, downed the entire glass of wine in one gulp. The bubbles went right up his nose and he began choking.

"Oh, dear!" Kitt set her glass on the bar, then put his up, too, and patted his back while Sean shoved a couple of paper towels at him.

Cheeks burning, Rye waited out the coughing fit, aware that the room had suddenly quieted and he and Kitt were the center of attention…again. Voice scratchy and barely above a whisper, he said, "Is there someplace we can go talk?"

Kitt glanced at Conor, who dipped his head toward the steps down to the wine cellar and shrugged off his fleece zip jacket. "Take this, Kitt, it's chilly down there."

The fiery sensation had migrated to the tips of Rye's ears as he followed Kitt to the stairs, his hand on her lower back where the beads on her dress tickled his palm. They made it all the way down the steps without incident and Rye heaved an inward sigh of relief. At least he hadn't tripped and tumbled them both down to the concrete floor, where one of her cousins would find them, broken and bloodied.

It was a start, and it was indeed damn chilly down in the wine cellar.

He took Conor's fleece jacket, prepared to lay it over her shoulders, but not before he stood back to gaze at her. "You…you are so incredibly beautiful." His voice was finally back, thank God. "That dress is sensational."

She blushed, her cheeks pinkening in the light shining from the small office nearby. "You look quite grand yourself,

Lieutenant."

Rye had dressed carefully for the evening in charcoal khakis, a dark gray button-down shirt, and his favorite wine-colored wool sweater. He smoothed a hand over the sweater. "It's the closest thing to red I own."

"It looks soft." She reached a hand toward him, then dropped it, appearing suddenly shy.

He caught her hand and placed her fingers on his chest, over his pounding heart. "It is. Feel."

She took a quick breath. "Your heart's beating awfully fast."

He studied the pulse showing just above her collarbone as he slipped the jacket over her shoulders. "So is yours."

"Aye." She nodded. "Ryker, I—"

"Wait. Before you say anything, please… This"—he swished one finger back and forth between them—"I want us to see if we can make it work." He snugged the front of the jacket around her, tugging her nearer in the process. They were so close he could feel her warm breath on his face, see the anticipation in her eyes. Ducking in, he framed her face with his hands and kissed her full on the lips before she could retreat.

To his utter amazement, she didn't even try to withdraw. Rather, she kissed him back, tilting her head to grant him access, and looping her arms around his neck. For few minutes, he was lost in her lips, her tongue seeking his, her fingers rumpling his hair. It was intoxicating. When he finally lifted his head, her mouth was red and swollen with kisses and her eyes shone with what he longed to define as more than lust.

"Kitt, I—"

She hushed him with one finger against his lips. "No, let me. Please?"

He nodded once, closed his fingers around her hand, and pressed a kiss into her palm. Her expression was so serious, his heart dropped to his socks. She was going to tell him she wouldn't take a chance on him. That she was too scared he'd hurt her. He ransacked his brain for the right words, but his mind went blank as she began to speak.

"You frighten me." She stroked his cheek. "*This* frightens me. I've never felt such fierce attraction to anyone before. Not even Ethan, who broke my heart so badly, I ne'er thought I'd survive. And here I am—achin' for *you* every moment of every day. Ah, what you do to me, Lieutenant... The fear and the longin' have been doin' battle inside me for only a few short weeks, yet I *know*. I know sure as we're standing here in each other's arms that I'd be a fool not to take a chance with you. And today I got this. It's a sign." She reached for the tiny bag on her hip and pulled out an envelope. "It's my work visa. I can stay."

Relief and elation washed over Rye so intensely that tears pricked his eyelids. He swallowed hard, not sure where to begin, so he simply plunged in, talking fast. "Recently, a very wise friend told me that real love is worth waiting for, even if you get your heart broken a little along the way. Without even knowing it, I've been breaking hearts, trying to prove that I wasn't exactly the kind of man I swore I'd never be. Yet I *was* that guy." He shrugged, slowing his words, determined to make her understand. "All the time, all I've really wanted is to love and be loved. You've opened my heart, Kathleen Boynton, and made me see who I truly am and I think I like *that* man. He's real. He's *good*. All I ask is that you trust me because I've never been so sure of anything before—you're the one I've been waiting for all my life. Can you trust me, Kitt?" His voice grew husky on the question and he swallowed hard again.

She gazed at him, her lower lip trembling in spite of the tears of joy shimmering in her eyes. "You *are* a good man, Ryker Lange. The kind of man I've always hoped to fall in love with." She kissed him then—a long, deep kiss full of passion and intention that left him breathless and longing for more. "Aye, Lieutenant, I trust you. Let's see if we make this work."

Rye grinned, finally releasing the last of his own trepidation in a huge contented sigh. "So, Irish, show me that letter from—" He stopped, listening, then grabbed her hand. "Well, crap on a cracker."

They followed the sounds of scuffling and shushing around the corner into the hallway. There on the stairwell was a clutch of townsfolk, Noah, Dot, Clyde and Gloria, several Flahertys, the Walker cousins, Harley Cole, and others who were out of sight on the steps above, peering over the banister into the dimness below. Even Jane stood on the fourth step in front of a guy Rye recognized but couldn't place and...

Holy cats, does that guy have his hands on Mom's shoulders?

That was certainly something to investigate later, but for

the moment, Rye tightened his grip on Kitt's hand and felt her shaking with silent laughter. "What the hell are you people doing?" he asked in his best gruff cop voice.

Looking deservedly sheepish, Noah glanced at the group behind him before clearing his throat. "Okay, you two...who won the bet?"

He glared at them just long enough to build some tension, then met Kitt's eyes. For a fraction of a moment, she was the only person in the room, her smile rendering him powerless to speak.

Then she kissed him, a kiss that told the whole town exactly what they wanted to know. When he lifted his head, the crowd clapped, whistled, and shouted, but his love murmured, "We both won, aye?"

Rye's heart soared. "Aye," he returned softly and bent his head for another delicious kiss.

The End

Want more? Check out Max and Lauren's story in
Falling for the Doctor!

Join Tule Publishing's newsletter for more great reads and weekly deals!

If you enjoyed *The Valentine Wager*,
you'll love the next book in…

The Lange Brothers series

Book 1: *The Valentine Wager*

Book 2: *Falling for the Doctor*
Coming in June 2022!

Available now at your favorite online retailer!

More books by Nan Reinhardt

The Four Irish Brothers Winery series

Book 1: *A Small Town Christmas*

Book 2: *Meant to Be*

Book 3: *Christmas with You*

Book 4: *The Baby Contract*

Available now at your favorite online retailer!

About the Author

Nan Reinhardt has been a copy editor and proofreader for over twenty-five years, and currently works mainly on fiction titles for a variety of clients, including Avon Books, St. Martin's Press, Kensington Books, Tule Publishing, and Entangled Publishing, as well as for many indie authors.

Author Nan writes romantic fiction for women in their prime. Yeah, women still fall in love and have sex, even after they turn forty-five! Imagine! She is also a wife, a mom, a mother-in-law, and a grandmother. She's been an antiques dealer, a bank teller, a stay-at-home mom, and a secretary.

She loves her career as a freelance editor, but writing is Nan's first and most enduring passion. She can't remember a time in her life when she wasn't writing—she wrote her first romance novel at the age of ten, a love story between the most sophisticated person she knew at the time, her older sister (who was in high school and had a driver's license!), and a member of Herman's Hermits. If you remember who they are, *you* are Nan's audience! She's still writing romance, but now from the viewpoint of a wiser, slightly rumpled, post-menopausal woman who believes that love never ages, women only grow more interesting, and everybody needs a little sexy romance.